BLOOD GOLD

n Patrick Grady and Rusty Anderton
: into Hangman's Gulch with a stash of
d filling their saddlebags, the last person
y want to see is the notorious bandit Jack
and when Jack ambushes them their
consolation is that he doesn't take their
: too. Patrick and Rusty vow to retrieve
d or die trying, but the news of their
tune has spread and now every man
un a hundred miles wants the gold for
elf. One hell of a fight is coming and
ever survives it sure will have earned a
of that gold!

BLOOD GOLD

BLOOD GOLD

by

Scott Connor

Dales Large Print Books
Long Preston, North Yorkshire,
BD23 4ND, England.

British Library Cataloguing in Publication Data.

Connor, Scott
    Blood gold.

A catalogue record of this book is
available from the British Library

ISBN   1-84262-440-7 pbk

First published in Great Britain 2005 by Robert Hale Limited

Copyright © Scott Connor 2005

Cover illustration © Faba by arrangement with
Norma Editorial S.A.

The right of Scott Connor to be identified as the author of this
work has been asserted by him in accordance with the
Copyright, Designs and Patents Act, 1988

Published in Large Print 2006 by arrangement with
Robert Hale Ltd.

Dales Large Print is an imprint of Library Magna Books Ltd.

Printed and bound in Great Britain by
T.J. (International) Ltd., Cornwall, PL28 8RW

CHAPTER 1

'Pick up the gun!' Jack Wolf roared.

For long moments Patrick Grady glared at Jack, then slowly lowered his head.

Ten feet before him on the rocky outcrop above Hangman's Gulch lay two guns. Twenty feet away stood his partner, Rusty Anderton.

Patrick snorted and stood tall.

'I ain't doing that,' he muttered.

Jack sauntered three slow paces to stand over the guns. A gust of wind blowing down the gulch whipped his coat as he glanced around the circle of bandits surrounding Patrick and Rusty. His single eye darted back and forth, the ruined wasteland of his other orbit red and angry.

Encouraging nods and eager grins rippled round the circle.

Jack kicked Patrick's gun. The weapon slammed into Patrick's right foot, but Patrick kept his gaze on Jack and smiled defiantly.

Jack snorted and kicked the other gun. It slid to a halt two feet in front of Rusty.

From the corner of his eye Patrick glanced at Rusty, who clutched his arms to his chest and stopped running his tongue through his moustache so that a timid smile could emerge.

'Like Patrick said,' Rusty murmured, his voice shaking, 'I ain't taking my gun either.'

'One way or another,' Jack muttered, pointing a firm finger at each man in turn, 'you two will entertain me. This way, one of you lives. The other way, you'll both be praying to die by sundown.'

The circle of bandits chuckled, the sound low and humourless.

'I'd sooner die the man I am,' Patrick spat, 'than kill my partner.'

Patrick glanced at Rusty, searching for more defiance, but Rusty had slammed a shaking hand over his eyes.

Jack backed three paces to stand beside the four saddlebags he'd just seized from Patrick and Rusty.

Inside the saddlebags were dozens of smaller bags, which, after nine months of successful prospecting, bulged with gold dust. But Patrick's and Rusty's streak of luck had ended when they'd taken what they thought was the safer route to Black Rock through Hangman's Gulch.

There, the bandit Jack Wolf had ambushed them.

After a short chase and skirmish, Jack had captured them and their gold. After some shoving and taunting, Jack had decided to have some fun. He'd returned Patrick's and Rusty's guns to them, each loaded with a single bullet, and ordered them to face each other in a fast draw showdown. And, as a torturous enticement, he'd promised them that the one who killed the other would go free, albeit substantially poorer than before.

'So,' Jack said, chuckling, 'you want a way

out, do you?'

Patrick shrugged. 'Yeah.'

Jack kicked a bag on its side, then glanced around his circle of men.

A cry started, low at first then growing with each repeated shout.

'Cards, cards, cards!' each bandit intoned, accompanying each cry with a clap of hands. 'Cards, cards, *cards.*'

Jack laughed. 'Sounds like it's time to ask the cards.'

Patrick and Rusty shared a bemused glance.

'What's that mean?' Patrick muttered.

Using two outstretched fingers, Jack extracted a battered pack of cards from his top jacket pocket and held them aloft.

'You draw a card. And that card decides your fate.' Jack patted the pack of cards, then tapped his chin. 'A non-face card says you fight the showdown. A two-eyed face card says you don't have to fight.' Jack glanced around, smirking. 'A one-eyed card says you keep your gold dust.'

'Hey,' Brady Hagen whined, 'we ain't siding with—'

Jack pointed a firm finger at Brady.

'Quiet. We live by the cards.'

'And I ain't siding with that either,' Patrick said as Brady lowered his head. 'Those ain't good odds.'

Jack ripped his gun from its holster and lifted it high, sighting Patrick's kneecap with his one good eye.

'If you don't take them, you can just die.' Jack licked his lips. 'And I've just thought of a way that'll take till long after sundown.'

Patrick gulped, but then jutted his chin and stood tall.

'As I said, I'll die the man I am rather than die entertaining scum.'

'Patrick,' Rusty said, rubbing a quivering hand over his damp brow. 'Just take a card.'

Patrick snorted. 'I ain't.'

'Just do it.' Rusty glanced down at the gun at his feet, then held his hands wide and flashed a half-smile. 'You might get lucky.'

Patrick hung his head a moment, then

took a deep breath. With a last glance at Rusty, and an encouraging nod from his partner, he strode up to Jack and extended an arm, then drew it back.

'So if I draw the king of diamonds, the jack of spades, or the jack of hearts, we keep our gold?'

Jack nodded and fanned the cards out, his one eye gleaming in the light from the high sun.

With his hand shaking with the slightest of tremors, Patrick half pulled a card from the pack.

He lifted a corner and snorted. While staring at Jack, he ripped the card from the pack and twisted it over.

Jack chuckled. 'So you get to fight that showdown, after all.'

Patrick flicked the three of spades on the ground and slammed his hands on his hips.

'What did that prove?'

'It put your fate into the cards. And the cards said that one of you lives and one of you dies.' Jack grabbed the card from the ground and slipped the pack into his pocket. 'The gun can decide which one.'

Patrick turned his back on Jack and edged towards his gun, shaking his head. He rolled his shoulders, then toed the gun to the side towards Rusty's gun. Still shaking his head, he shuffled to it and toed it another foot.

As a murmured grumbling started from Jack's men, Patrick bent and extended a hand to grab the gun, but he stopped with his fingers just brushing the metal.

Rusty gulped and knelt beside his gun.

Jack and his men chuckled at Patrick's and Rusty's submission. Bets changed hands, most backing Patrick to win the showdown.

But as Rusty grabbed his gun, Patrick fumbled with his gun and as he rooted on the ground for it, he leaned towards Rusty.

'That Jack Wolf ain't living long enough to enjoy our gold,' he whispered to Rusty. 'I'll take him. You take whoever you like.'

Rusty winced. 'And then what? We've only got one bullet apiece.'

'We take our chances.' Patrick looked

around the solid circle of grinning bandits. He counted fifteen. 'But whatever you do, do it fast and keep moving.'

'That'll just get us killed.'

'Everything we do will just get–'

'Be quiet, you two!' Jack roared. He folded his arms and grinned. 'It's time for the showdown.'

Patrick darted a last harsh glare at Rusty, then stood and holstered his gun. He paced back to leave five clear yards between himself and Rusty, then hunched down, hoping that he was adopting a gunslinger crouch.

Facing him, Rusty matched his actions, but his hands were shaking even more than before and his gaze darted around the circle of grinning men. Patrick stared at Rusty until he looked at him. While moving his lips as little as he dared, he mouthed a countdown.

Ten.

Patrick directed an encouraging smile at Rusty.

Nine.

Rusty frowned so deeply his face seemed to cave in.

Eight.

Patrick rolled his shoulders and blew on his fingers.

Seven.

Rusty gulped and rubbed his sweating palms on his jacket.

Six.

Patrick settled his stance.

Five.

Rusty jabbed his shaking fingers through his thick red beard.

Four.

Patrick glanced to the side, noting Jack's exact position ten yards to his left.

Three.

Rusty closed his eyes a moment, his mouth moving feverishly as he mouthed a benediction.

Two.

Patrick stood tall and took a deep breath.

One.

Rusty stared deep into Patrick's eyes. His

head waggled in the shortest of shakes.

Zero.

Patrick whirled his hand to his holster and turned on the hip towards Jack. But then hot fire punched into his guts, knocking him back and around, his pained finger-twitch gouging his only bullet into the earth scant inches before Jack's feet.

He staggered a pace, then dropped to his knees, clutching his guts, and toppled on to his side. Through pain-racked eyes, he looked up.

In his outstretched hand, Rusty had aimed his shaking gun straight at Patrick. A flurry of smoke rose from the gun barrel.

Rusty shook his head, his eyes wide and beseeching.

'It wasn't me,' he screeched.

Patrick opened his mouth to scream a denial, but darkness claimed him.

CHAPTER 2

Light ripped into Patrick's eyes, then faded to oblivion. Pain besieged Patrick, but stayed.

The fire in his guts burned, enveloping his mind.

He tried to shout for help, but he couldn't force words from the blasted desert that was his mouth.

But that wasn't the worst of it.

Whenever he almost dragged himself back to reality, he thought that someone had bound him and hung him upside down. And worse, he steadily swayed back and forth.

Through intense willpower, he forced himself awake to find he was lying over a horse, the ground just feet below him. But the apparent swaying of the ground forced a vomiting attack from his tortured body.

The muscle spasms ripped his insides and this time, he welcomed the darkness that came and stayed.

'How are you feeling?'

The question came from a woman.

Patrick tried to croak an answer, but no words emerged. With a gritty gulp, he cleared his throat and forced his eyes to open.

A plain face peered down at him, but the eyes were kind and young.

Patrick instructed his head to turn, but his vision remained fixed on the face. With just his eyes, he glanced around.

He was in a room, ornately furnished, but decayed and reeking of incense. He glanced down. He lay on a bed, dressed in just his underclothes, a single blanket folded back across his midriff. Bandages encased his chest. They were clean with no blood showing.

'Who are you?' he croaked.

'Hannah, Hannah Foster. And how are you feeling?'

Patrick forced his hand to lift from his side and tentatively poked his bandages.

'I don't know. How am I feeling?'

Hannah provided a kind smile. 'If you don't know, I'd better let Gideon advise you.'

'Just tell me the truth.' Patrick raised his eyebrows. 'You are a nurse, aren't you?'

'No. I'm a...' Hannah's eyes appeared to glaze a moment. She shook her head with the barest of movements. 'I'm not a nurse.'

Patrick lunged and gripped Hannah's arm.

'Just tell me if I'll live.'

Hannah flinched, but instead of attempting to remove his hand, she laid her other hand on his brow.

'I reckon so. If anyone can help you, Gideon Law can.'

'Is he a doctor?'

'Yeah. He's the best.'

'Glad you think so,' a man said from Patrick's side.

Patrick released Hannah's arm and forced

his head to turn.

A man, far younger than Patrick expected, smiled at him from the doorway – Gideon Law.

'What happened?' Patrick asked.

'Someone shot you. That's what happened. But I removed the bullet without too much trouble.' Gideon smiled. 'And to answer the question you were asking Hannah – you'll live. The bullet cracked a rib, but it didn't cause as much damage as it might have. If you rest for a week or two, you'll mend. In a month, you'll be back to your old self.'

'I can't rest.' Patrick looked to the ceiling and breathed deeply through his nostrils, forcing down the burst of anger that threatened to cloud his vision. 'I have to ... to find someone.'

Gideon sauntered to Patrick's bedside and busied himself with prodding at Patrick's dressing.

'Good work, Hannah. You have a real skill here.' He flashed Hannah a smile, then glanced down at Patrick. 'You can do all the *finding* you need to do once you've healed. For now, you aren't going anywhere.'

Patrick thrust an arm down to his side and tried to lever himself up, but as he only shifted an inch, he flopped into the cushions and decided to accept advice.

'And where is here?' he asked, now enveloped in the cushioned bed.

'This is Destitution.' Gideon glanced around the room. 'And you're in the Belle Starr.'

'A hotel?'

Gideon winced. 'No. A whorehouse.'

'Thanks for reminding me,' Hannah said. She forced a thin smile and turned to the door. 'I have to go.'

CHAPTER 3

Deep within his mind, hatred burned Patrick's soul with one desire– Kill Rusty. That thought blasted and echoed in his mind, drowning out all rational considerations.

But after two failed attempts to roll out of bed and two sharp pains ripping through his chest, he relented and let sleep overcome him.

From time to time he awoke and, from the passage of the rectangle of light cast by the window on to the floor and the varying levels of commotion beyond the door, he could tell that another day started, passed, and ended.

On a regular basis, Hannah and Gideon called in on him. They changed his dressings and fed him, but they studiously ignored his repeated questions about when he could move on.

Early in the afternoon, Hannah returned.

'How can I pay for my care?' Patrick asked, broaching the subject of when he could leave from a different angle.

'You don't have to. It's been paid for.'

'Who?'

Hannah winced. 'Perhaps I should fetch Gideon to explain.'

'No. Just tell me. Who's paying for my care?'

Hannah backed a pace, but then glanced to her side and frowned.

The door swung fully open to reveal Rusty Anderton standing in the doorway. He paced into the room, nibbling on his bottom lip.

'I'm paying,' he said. He wrung his hands, then held them wide. 'And it took everything that Jack Wolf and his bandits didn't take.'

'You!' Patrick roared, flinging up a hand to point at Rusty.

Rusty shrugged and hung his head a

moment. He glanced at Hannah, then at the door.

Hannah nodded and edged around Rusty to the door and outside, but her footfalls halted three paces down the corridor.

'Glad you're mending,' Rusty said. 'When I looked in on you yesterday, you looked terrible.'

'That's because you shot me,' Patrick grunted, 'you low-down–'

'I didn't shoot you.'

'You fired. I got lead in the guts.'

'We've been through too much over the last year.' Rusty paced across the room and leaned on Patrick's bed. He peered at the bandages and smiled. 'I'd never hurt you.'

'Then how come I had a bullet in me?'

'One of Jack's bandits shot you. It wasn't–'

'Liar!'

Patrick lunged, his clawing swipe grabbing Rusty's throat. With all his strength he squeezed, but Rusty just placed his hand over Patrick's hand and lifted it from his neck.

'Rest, Patrick. You're still far weaker than

you think you are. We'll talk about this when you get your strength back.'

Rusty turned and paced from Patrick's bed. In the doorway he glanced back, a wan smile splitting his thick red beard, then shuffled outside.

From the corridor, Patrick heard Rusty's and Hannah's low voices muttering. With a supreme effort, Patrick threw back the blanket covering him and swung his legs to the floor. He stood, but his legs folded and he plummeted to the floor, landing in a sprawling heap.

Rusty dashed in, Hannah at his heels.

'Get away from me,' Patrick muttered from the floor.

Rusty rocked on his heels, but Hannah shook her head.

'Just get Gideon,' she said. 'We'll sort him out.'

One last time, Rusty glanced down at Patrick, then nodded and dashed outside, leaving Hannah staring at Patrick, shaking her head.

'You're a bull-headed idiot, Patrick,' she said.

'You ain't the first to say that.'

Patrick threw out a hand and dragged himself a clawed yard nearer to the doorway, but pain ripped through his chest and, unable to control his movements, he flopped on his side.

When Gideon clattered into the room, he and Hannah levered an arm under each armpit and helped him into bed. Throughout, Patrick listened to their admonishments, and replied with sullen agreements. But Rusty's treachery had taken root in his mind and was thrusting revengeful tendrils into every fibre of his being.

When his two carers eventually trusted him enough to leave him, he lay back and stared at the ceiling. But he'd started counting.

When he judged that thirty minutes had passed, he pushed back the blanket and swung his legs to the floor.

He sat a moment, willing the dizziness to

depart, then rolled forward. On his feet, he straightened as much as he could then tottered back and forth, but his legs supported him. Smiling now, he shuffled across the floor to the window and peered outside, confirming that he was on the first floor.

The sun was high and other than a row of horses tethered outside the saloon, Destitution's only road was deserted.

He shuffled to the door, levered it open an inch, and peered through the gap. Nobody was in the corridor. Only subdued chatter from the saloon drifted up the stairs.

Then, having completed the maximum he thought he could achieve for his first real foray out of bed, he rolled back into bed.

Each half-hour, he repeated this exercise, and each time he was quicker, the dizziness was less, his stride was more confident and, best of all, he learned how to avoid damaging his chest. The wound only throbbed with a dull ache.

On his fourth journey he rummaged through the drawers, finding his clothing in one and a cudgel in another. He grinned and secreted the weapon beneath his bed-clothes beside his right leg.

Late in the afternoon, Gideon looked in on him.

'You're looking brighter,' he said.

Patrick nodded. 'I feel brighter.'

'In that case you can answer a question.' Gideon slammed his hands on his hips. 'What in tarnation did you think you were doing attacking Rusty?'

Patrick jutted his chin. 'That ain't your concern.'

'Rusty saved your life, but you tried to strangle him.'

'It's between him and me.' Patrick took a deep breath and fingered the cudgel. He forced his shoulders to slump and provided his most disarming smile. 'But I get hot-headed sometimes. And I've thought things through. Perhaps if Rusty still wants to see me, I'll be more reasonable.'

'Glad to hear it. But you won't get the chance. Rusty just left town. He left you this.' Gideon extracted a wad of bills from his pocket and held them out to Patrick, but as Patrick just glared at them, he dropped them on the bed. 'I've already taken a cut for your care.'

Patrick released his grip on the cudgel and with an outstretched finger, riffled through the bills, counting over fifty dollars.

'Where did he get this? Jack left us with nothing.'

'He didn't say.'

'Thanks, I suppose.' Patrick slotted the cash under the pillow. 'Suppose he's going after Jack Wolf. As will I as soon as you stop doctoring me.'

'In your state you can't take on the likes of that bandit.'

Patrick furrowed his brow and leaned forward as far as his encased chest would allow.

'How come you know about him?'

'Last week Jack rested up in Destitution. He got into a fight with another lowlife, Salvador Milano. He'd have killed Salvador if that varmint hadn't have got himself some sense and run. Then Jack headed north, where he met you when you were unlucky enough to be heading south. I didn't see him, but from what I heard, he isn't someone I'd risk arguing with, however much gold he stole from me.'

'Ain't looking for your advice.' Patrick lay back and closed his eyes.

Gideon stood over him a moment, tutting, then left the room.

Patrick listened to Gideon's footsteps recede down the corridor, then threw back the blanket.

He shuffled to the drawers and removed his clothes. With care he dressed, discovering that he had to stay hunched to avoid the painful results of stretching.

He edged to the door and outside, keeping his back to the wall as he sidled down the corridor. At the balcony, he peered into the saloon below.

At the bar, several customers were hunched over coffee mugs, but as none of them was either Gideon or Hannah, he slipped down the side of the stairs and straight outside.

His guts throbbed with every shuffled pace down the boardwalk, but he had errands to run.

'Patrick, you bull-headed idiot,' Gideon muttered. He pushed the drawer closed and stood with his hands on his hips a moment, considering the abandoned bed, then sauntered to the window.

He peered up and down the road, and just as he was about to turn away he saw Patrick hobble from the store, a bulging saddlebag on his shoulder, a shining Colt on his hip. Patrick mounted a horse. In the saddle, he flinched and hunched over, clutching his guts, then inch by inch righted himself.

Gideon sighed, then hurried from the room and down the corridor and stairs. Outside, as he dashed across the boardwalk, Patrick was lifting the reins with his gaze set on the edge of town.

Gideon paced into the road and stood

before Patrick.

'Had a feeling you wouldn't listen to advice,' he muttered, raising his arms.

'You can't stop me leaving,' Patrick grunted, staring over Gideon's shoulder at the plains beyond.

'I can't, but as your doctor, I'm advising you to stay here and rest for at least another week.'

Patrick snorted and lifted the reins high.

'As a patient who's paid his bills, I got no reason to stay when I got gold to find.'

Gideon sighed. 'Nothing I can say will stop you leaving, but there's a chance you won't live long enough to find anything but death. Too much movement could open up that wound and with nobody to patch you up...'

Patrick tipped his hat, then pulled on the reins.

'You're right. Nothing you can say will stop me leaving.'

Patrick sidled his horse past Gideon, then without a backward glance, trotted from Destitution.

Standing in the centre of the road, Gideon watched Patrick leave town; he shook his head. Then he turned and with his head down, sauntered towards the Belle Starr.

From the shadows in the alley beside the Belle Starr, Salvador Milano stepped out, his eyes lively and the usual arrogant smirk plastered across his grimed face.

Gideon flinched, then shrugged and moved to walk past him, but Salvador jumped to the side and threw both his arms back to hold on to the swing-doors and block Gideon's way. He rocked back and forth, licking his lips.

'Now that sure was an interestin' conversation,' he drawled.

Gideon shrugged. 'If you reckon so.'

'I do.' Salvador chuckled. 'And I reckon I might just buy you and me a right friendly drink while you explain it to me.'

Gideon opened his mouth to mutter a refusal, but with a last glance over his shoulder at the small and distant form of Patrick riding into the plains, he nodded and let Salvador shepherd him into the saloon.

CHAPTER 4

At the bar in the Belle Starr, Salvador Milano hunched over his second whiskey.

'Who attacked 'em?' he grunted.

Gideon swirled his whiskey, then gulped it.

'Jack Wolf and his bandit gang.'

'So,' Salvador mused, 'Jack's now got himself a whole mess o' gold.'

Salvador licked his lips and knocked back the remainder of his whiskey.

Gideon considered Salvador's sly smirk for a moment, then snorted.

'Hope you aren't thinking of going after that gold. You know what he did to you last week.'

'I know that.' Salvador rubbed his jaw, the bruising now yellowed and fading. He nodded slowly. 'I'm just musin'. Where did

Jack ambush 'em?'

'Hangman's Gulch.' As Salvador shrugged, Gideon pointed through the window. 'It's about thirty miles out. You head—'

Salvador lifted a hand. 'Quit talkin'. You'll take me there.'

'I want nothing to do with this.'

Gideon lifted his whiskey, but with a lightning gesture, Salvador grabbed his arm, halting his hand with the glass brushing his lips.

'Take me there.' Salvador widened his eyes and with his other hand, patted his holster.

Gideon glanced at the holster and shrugged.

'All right. I'll take you to the gulch, but no further.'

Salvador lifted his hand from Gideon's arm.

'Once I got me Jack's trail, I got no use for you.'

'Reckoned you might want my help. Once you find Jack, he'll fill you so full of holes, you'll need me to fill them.' Gideon sipped his whiskey, then chuckled. 'Or perhaps just someone to bury you.'

'You're either brave for jestin' me, or stupid,' Salvador muttered, his right eye twitching. 'Which are you?'

'Neither,' Gideon said, setting his earnest gaze on Salvador. 'I'm just telling you the truth.'

For long moments Salvador glared at Gideon, but as Gideon continued to stare back, he nodded and hung his head a moment.

'Perhaps you're talkin' sense. I need me an advantage to get Jack.' Salvador tapped his chin. Then a slow smile emerged. 'And I know where I'll get one.'

With an arrogant flick of the finger, he tipped his hat to Gideon and swaggered across the saloon to the stairs. He mounted the stairs three at a time, turned, then stalked along the upstairs corridor.

Belle Starr emerged from the shadows, her powdered, chubby face wreathed in a huge smile, which died as soon as she saw Salvador.

'I told you last week that you're banned from coming up here,' she muttered. 'Your custom ain't welcome until I say so.'

'Where's Hannah?' Salvador grunted.

'In the end room, but she's got company and you ain't seeing her either now or when she ain't got company.'

'I got money,' Salvador snarled.

'You may have. And when you treat my girls right, they treat you right back. Gideon patched up Sally and she'll be fine, but you charging up here just proves you ain't learnt your lesson.' Belle set her squat legs wide and bunched her shoulders. 'You take one pace past me, and you ain't welcome in here ever again.'

Salvador licked his lips, then brushed past Belle.

'You wouldn't dare.'

'George!' Belle screamed, but Salvador continued his firm pacing down the corridor to the end room.

In front of the door, Salvador rolled his shoulders, then kicked open the door.

'Hey,' a voice cried from the bed. 'What you...'

A flushed face peered over the bedclothes and stared at Salvador, then gulped.

'Get out while you can still walk,' Salvador muttered, tucking a thumb in his gunbelt.

The man leapt from the bed and dashed to the door, gathering his clothes with frantic haste. He edged past Salvador, not meeting his eyes, then hurtled down the corridor, pausing only to shuffle into his trousers and gather sufficient decency. But when he'd clattered to the end of the corridor, he yelled for Belle.

With the bedclothes hitched to her chin, Hannah glared at Salvador from the bed.

'I've heard about you from Sally,' she muttered. 'I ain't going with you.'

Salvador snorted and took a long pace into the room.

'You'll do whatever I pay for.'

As Hannah jutted her chin and glared at Salvador with steady defiance, firm footfalls paced down the corridor to the end room.

'That's enough, Salvador,' Belle said from the doorway.

Salvador turned to face Belle.

As ever when trouble threatened to erupt, Silent George stood behind her, looming a good two feet above her head. His bony, bald head and wide eyes gleamed as he cracked his knuckles.

'Like I said,' Salvador muttered, 'I got money.'

Belle glanced over her shoulder at George, then shrugged.

'I like money.' She smiled. But the smile died and a harsh glare took its place. 'But sometimes, it just ain't worth it.'

'For the right price what you provide is always available.'

Salvador reached into his jacket pocket. With his gaze never moving from Belle's eyes, he counted bills into his other hand.

When twenty dollars accumulated, Belle edged from foot to foot. At thirty dollars, she bit her bottom lip. At forty, she mopped her brow.

At fifty, she whistled and with a flash of a thin-lipped smile at Hannah, she held out her hand.

'All right,' she said. 'What do you want for that kind of money?'

'You got yourself the right idea, Belle. I want Hannah, for a week.'

Belle closed her eyes a moment, then nodded.

'She's yours,' she whispered.

Salvador glanced at Hannah and sneered.

'Then get her cleaned up and ready to leave town at sun-up.'

'I ain't–' Hannah screeched, but Belle raised an imperious hand, quietening her.

Belle took a deep breath. 'What you planning to do with her for a week?'

'That ain't none of your concern.' Salvador snorted and moved to leave the room, but Belle planted a finger on Salvador's shoulder and traced it down his sleeve.

'But Hannah's plain, scrawny, and hardly worth fifty dollars,' she whispered with a flutter of eyelashes. 'Perhaps one of my other girls might be more to your liking – and one who *can* deal with you. Unless you ain't man enough to deal with a real woman.'

Salvador shrugged from the tracing finger. 'I just want Hannah for a week.'

Belle glanced over her shoulder at Silent George, then turned back, her painted eyebrows raised, her stern expression back.

'And I want her back in a week in one piece, understand?'

Salvador slammed the fifty dollars into Belle's hand.

'And I've paid for her, understand?'

'Ain't objecting.' With a practised flick of her wrist, the money disappeared. 'I just didn't think Hannah had caught your eye.'

'She ain't.' Salvador glanced at Hannah and snorted. 'But she's caught someone else's.'

As the rumour of the gold Jack Wolf had stolen from Patrick and Rusty had ripped through Destitution in a matter of minutes, Salvador Milano easily rounded up nine men who were enthusiastic enough, or drunk enough, to reckon they could reclaim it from Jack.

After two short squabbles and one near gunfight, Salvador took control of the men and the next day, an hour before sun-up, a line of riders trotted from Destitution and headed into the hills towards Hangman's Gulch.

Five riders scouted around at the front and another four stayed back, leaving Gideon and Hannah riding two horses lengths behind Salvador in the centre.

They rode in sullen silence, but as the first sliver of sun poked above the hills, Hannah speeded to ride alongside Salvador.

'Why am I here?' she muttered.

'You're a whore,' Salvador spat. 'Jack got mighty attached to you. Figure out the rest yourself.'

Hannah held her chin aloft. 'I ain't got a dirty mind like you. You'll have to tell me.'

Salvador gripped the reins more tightly, his jaw bunched.

'You'll keep Jack all happy and distracted while his gold disappears.'

Hannah snorted. 'So you plan to find Jack and give me to him, then he'll be so pleased, he'll drop his guard and you'll take his gold?'

Salvador grinned and spat a long gob of spit to the side.

'Yup. For a whore you got yourself some brains.'

'But I'm no sneak. I'm a whore, like you said.'

Salvador patted his holster. 'If you won't sneak, you can decide if you want to be a dead whore, or a live whore.'

Hannah glanced away from Salvador's lively grin and slowed her horse to edge back from him. Salvador watched her until she'd dropped back enough to ride beside Gideon, then faced the front, but from the way that he rocked his head from side to side, Gideon reckoned he was still grinning.

'I heard that,' Gideon said, his voice low. 'And you don't have to do this.'

'I got no choice.' Hannah glared ahead at Salvador's back. 'He paid for me.'

'But it was just fifty dollars.' Gideon lifted his free hand a moment to hold both hands wide. 'And you won't even see that money.'

Hannah stared straight ahead. 'Belle will do all right by me.'

'If you live.'

'I'll live.' Hannah turned to stare at Gideon with her lips set in a smile that was harsher than Gideon had ever seen from her. 'Women who willingly provide something men want tend to survive.'

Gideon gulped. 'But you could be so much more.'

'Like what?' she snapped. 'Ain't nothing for the likes of me in a town like Destitution.'

'Last week, you helped me patch up Sally. And you cared for Patrick Grady with some skill.'

'That was just a few bandages. It didn't take much effort.'

'It didn't – for you. Nursing is a skill and

not everyone can do it. You have a kind face, a gentle touch and an aptitude for caring.'

Hannah lowered her gaze a moment.

'You offering to pay for my help?'

Gideon rocked his head from side to side, then shook it.

'I'm sorry. I can't. But I could teach you more about doctoring and then you could go to a real town like Black Rock. And maybe there you could get work that's more suited to you than ... than...' Gideon choked on his last word and instead forced a smile.

Hannah muttered a short sigh. She turned to face the front and they returned to quietness.

As the sun edged away from the horizon, they approached Hangman's Gulch. Gideon hollered to Salvador and pointed at the deep ravine.

After ten minutes of scouting around, Gideon discovered footprints milling around a flat length of rock, which jutted into the gulch. Salvador agreed that this was probably where Jack had forced Patrick and

Rusty to fight their showdown.

Despite the mess of hoof-prints heading in all directions away from this rock, Mack Hoffer – one of the more resourceful men whom Salvador had recruited – untangled a concentrated set of trails leading away from the gulch and pointing north.

Salvador gathered everybody around him and barked instructions for them to follow Jack. He received a ripple of eager nods and the men mounted their horses.

With the side of his hand, Salvador tipped his hat to Gideon and grunted his thanks, then turned and headed north.

Throughout the searching of the area, Hannah hadn't dismounted and as Salvador turned to head away, she flashed Gideon a wan smile.

'Be seeing you,' she whispered.

Gideon opened his mouth to offer encouragement, but then closed it and returned a smile instead.

As Hannah hurried on ahead, Gideon mounted his horse and turned towards

Destitution, then turned back to watch the line of riders snake into the barren plains.

Just as they disappeared behind a large rocky outcrop, Hannah glanced over her shoulder and looked at Gideon.

Then they were gone.

Although Hannah's face had been too distant for Gideon to discern an expression, her hunched, defeated posture made his throat tighten.

For long moments Gideon sat hunched forward in the saddle, watching the deserted trail. Then, with a sigh, he lifted the reins and at a steady pace followed Salvador's group.

CHAPTER 5

For six hours Gideon Law followed Salvador's and Jack's trail at a slow trot, ensuring he kept well back from Salvador and his men.

He had no plan in mind.

Rejoining Salvador's group would lead to questions to which he didn't have answers and staying back gave him no chance of helping Hannah.

But he just had to keep going and hope something might happen and that he'd be in a position where he could help her.

In late afternoon he was riding through a stream when he saw a saddled horse chomping grass on the bank. Within seconds, he recognized it as the docile bay that Patrick had bought.

Gideon winced and peered down the length of the stream, but only saw the trees lining the bank. He dismounted and tethered his horse then, surprising himself with his luck, secured Patrick's bay at the first attempt.

Then he scouted downstream.

A quarter-mile or so on, he stopped and, judging that an injured Patrick wouldn't have strayed that far, he turned and headed back. Only fifty yards upstream from Patrick's bay, he saw a hunched form, lying in the shade of an old oak.

He dashed to Patrick's side and rolled him on his back.

Through narrowed eyes, Patrick stared at him, then yawned.

Gideon felt Patrick's brow. It was cool, but he ripped open his shirt. The bandages beneath still tightly bound his chest and no blood had seeped through.

Patrick opened his eyes wide.

'Howdy,' he croaked.

Gideon dashed to his horse, returned with a water canteen, and sprinkled water over Patrick's lips. Within a few dribbles, Patrick grabbed the canteen and gulped three long mouthfuls.

'What happened?' Gideon asked, rolling back on his haunches.

Patrick replaced the stopper in the canteen and wiped his mouth with the back of his hand.

'Some riders were following me. I didn't stop to find out if they were looking for me and galloped on. I hid by this stream until they'd passed.' Patrick yawned. 'But then that damn sun was hot and I just reckoned sleep sounded a mighty fine idea.'

'It is. After suffering a gunshot wound like you did, you need rest and plenty of it.'

'I can't afford the time.' Patrick pushed himself to a sitting position. 'I have to keep going.'

Gideon snorted. 'A man in your state *can* keep going, but when he gets to where he's going, he won't be much use to anyone.'

Patrick stretched, suppressing a wince by biting his lip.

'I can take on anybody.'

'I doubt that. But that isn't the worst of your problems now. Salvador Milano is after Jack too.'

'I don't care about that,' Patrick snapped. 'Now quit staring at me as if I'm about to die and help me to my horse.'

Gideon clutched Patrick's shoulders and dragged him to his feet, then swung him round and marched him to his horse. He stood back while Patrick mounted it, then mounted his own horse. But already Patrick was riding from the stream and back to the trail, gradually straightening with each stride.

Gideon hurried on to draw alongside.

'You mind if I ride along with you?' he asked.

'Trail is free.' Patrick turned in the saddle. 'And why are you out here?'

Gideon turned from Patrick to stare straight ahead.

'Salvador Milano made me show him where Jack ambushed you.'

'Hangman's Gulch is miles back. Why ain't you heading back to Destitution?'

Gideon considered a moment, then shrugged.

'I'm not sure.'

Patrick snorted. 'It'd better not be to doctor me.'

'It isn't.'

'Good. Because I've paid my bill and I'm plumb out of money to pay for more of your services.' Patrick uttered a low chuckle.

Gideon chuckled too. 'But being as you

mentioned doctoring, you prepared to take some advice?'

'Nope.' Patrick glared at the trail ahead, his slight show of humour gone from his firm-jawed expression.

Gideon opened his mouth to offer it anyhow, then shrugged and closed it.

In silence the two men rode west for a mile or so. But pace by pace the silence and Gideon's bemusement as to why he was still heading after Salvador dragged on his nerves, and he turned to Patrick.

'You mind if we talk?' he asked.

'Won't that sap my strength?'

'No, of course...' Gideon chuckled on seeing that Patrick was smiling. 'No, talking will be just fine.'

'What you want to talk about?'

Gideon rubbed his chin. 'You got family?'

'Everyone has family.'

'Not everyone.'

'True. And what about you? You have that nurse to go home to?'

'Hannah isn't a nurse,' Gideon snapped,

then softened his voice. 'She works at the Belle Starr.'

'What difference does that make?'

'None, I suppose.' Gideon sighed. 'But she isn't in Destitution. Salvador took her with him. He reckons she'll help him get Jack.'

Patrick nodded and glanced at Gideon from the corner of his eye.

'At least I now know for sure that you ain't here to doctor me.'

'I'm not sure if she's the reason why I'm heading after Salvador.'

'You may not be sure, but I am.' Patrick licked his lips and grinned. 'I may have been in the wilderness with just Rusty and my horse for company for the last year, but I recognized the way you looked at her.'

'Perhaps you're right,' Gideon whispered as he rubbed his brow. 'But you haven't said if you have anyone to go home to.'

'Unless you ain't figured it out yet – I ain't talking about it.'

Gideon edged his horse in towards Patrick.

'We might have a few days' riding ahead of us. We can spend that time quiet, but talking might make the time pass more quickly.'

Patrick snorted. 'My tale ain't that savoury.'

'Patrick, I get my custom from either Belle Starr's girls or their customers. In my ten years in Destitution, I've seen things that you'd never believe. Nothing can shock me.'

Patrick shrugged. 'It ain't anything as bad as that. I got fine children and a good wife, but for some reason, I got to drinking. Then I got to drinking even more.'

'But you don't drink now?'

'Nope. I met a man who planned to prospect for gold. Didn't sound like it stood a chance, but a year spent miles from whiskey seemed a way to sort myself out. And when I get an idea in my head, nobody can shake me from it.'

'I've seen.'

'So Rusty and me dug for gold. And we found gold. And I was just figuring that I could return home with money and rejoin my family when Jack ambushed me. Now, I won't have anything to give them unless I find Jack.'

'It isn't my place to say, but if your family lost a drunken man, they'll be mighty pleased to get back a sober man, even if he has no gold.'

'You're right,' Patrick snapped. 'It ain't your place to say that.'

'What're we going to do?' Don Ritter asked.

Jack Wolf glanced down the trail, then into the hills. He smiled.

For the last two days Jack's bandits had camped out, enjoying their new rich feeling and anticipating just what being rich would bring them.

As always when a big decision loomed, Jack had distanced himself from his men and had sat in contemplative silence on the edge of the site, but now he'd returned.

Jack pulled the pack of cards from his top pocket.

As one, his men smiled and started the chant.

'Cards, cards, cards.' They clapped their hands. 'Cards, cards, *cards.*'

Jack held the cards aloft.

'A non-face card says we'll be cautious and hide out at Fort Clemency for a month. A two-eyed card says we forget caution. We head for Denver and spend the money in a wild spree.'

Cliff Seals whooped with delight, several others joining him.

'I sure like the sound of that,' he said.

Jack nodded. 'A one-eyed card says we scatter the gold dust to the wind.'

Cliff's whooping died in an instant. He glanced around, receiving a ripple of gulps and shaking heads. Cliff shared a glance with Fernando Kimball. They both edged back and slipped a thumb behind their gunbelts. Even Leland Ashley, Jack's most loyal follower, mopped his brow.

Jack held the pack of cards at arm's length, then angled them in to his chest and fanned them out.

With a lunge, he ripped a card from the

pack. He glanced at it, then turned on the spot, showing everyone the ten of spades. A round of relieved sighs followed everyone's first sighting of the card. Then he returned it to the pack and slotted the pack into his top pocket.

'Fort Clemency it is. Saddle up.' Jack waved a hand above his head, then headed for his horse. 'We have ourselves a destination.'

'This is ridiculous,' Cliff shouted. 'We can't decide everything with those damn cards.'

'Hey,' Leland shouted. 'Jack has done all right by us so far. I see no reason to change things.'

'We have done fine. But now that we got ourselves some gold, I reckon we should decide what we do next and not just let Jack ask the cards.'

Jack grunted and turned his one-eyed glare on Cliff.

'You questioning my methods?'

Cliff gulped and backed a pace. 'I ain't doing that. I just–'

'You just, what?' Jack roared, spit flying

57

from his mouth.

Cliff took a deep breath. 'I just reckon I've had enough of playing the odds. If you'd drawn a one-eyed card, we'd have lost everything.'

'Two days ago, I asked the cards what our next destination should be and the four of clubs said we should head to Hangman's Gulch. Everything we gained there came from the cards.'

'It did. But then, we had nothing. Now, we got everything, and we got no reason to gamble any more.'

'When you have everything, gambling is all you have left.' Jack advanced a long pace and glared down at Cliff. 'And nobody follows me who doesn't support the cards. You're leaving.'

'I didn't say I wanted to go,' Cliff whined.

'You didn't. But I reckoned you might want to live.' Jack grinned, then slammed a fist into Cliff's jaw that sent him sprawling. Even before Cliff had slid to a halt, Jack had ripped his gun from its holster and aimed it down at Cliff's head. 'And I decided that without asking the cards.'

Cliff rubbed his jaw as he glared up at Jack, but then his shoulders slumped and he glanced around the semicircle of men.

'All right,' he murmured. 'Who's with me?'

Fernando strode three paces to stand alongside him.

Tort Rhine edged towards him a pace, then shuffled back.

'Anybody else?' Jack muttered. He roved his gun back and forth, receiving a wave of headshaking, then ripped a card from his top pocket and glanced at it. His one eye twitched as he slipped the card back into his pocket then holstered his gun. 'Seems as there ain't. Now go.'

With his gaze on Cliff, Jack stalked to the bags of gold and rummaged inside. He extracted four small bags and hurled them to Cliff's side.

Cliff sighed in relief and grabbed the bags, then rolled to his feet and tossed two to

Fernando. Then they backed to their horses. One by one they mounted them and backed away from Jack. When they were fifty yards away, with a last holler, they charged down the hillside.

The remainder of the gang also mounted their horses, but Jack stayed back and glared at Leland until he joined him.

'You happy with Cliff and Fernando leaving?' he asked.

Leland rocked his head from side to side.

'Suppose I ain't.' He shrugged. 'But if they want to go, we don't need men who don't accept your methods.'

Jack raised his eyebrows and lowered his voice.

'But I ain't happy with that gold getting away. Get it back.'

'I ain't doing that. I liked Cliff and Fernando.'

Jack grabbed Leland's arm. For long moments he glared at Leland with his one good eye, but as Leland returned his own firm gaze, he nodded. With his other hand,

60

he slipped the cards from his top pocket.

'The cards can decide. A low card says you get the gold. A–'

'No,' Leland snapped, ripping his arm from Jack's hand. 'This time I ain't accepting those odds.'

'Surely *you* ain't questioning my methods?'

'Not the methods, just the odds. You always give what you want to do the greatest chance. Well, this time, I want the odds for what I want to do to be the greatest.'

Jack shrugged. 'All right. A low card says Cliff and Fernando can leave. A two-eyed card says you'll get the gold back.' Jack rubbed his chin. 'A one-eyed card says I'll kill you for your impudence.'

As Leland gulped and backed a pace, Jack rolled his shoulders then, with a lunge, ripped a card from the pack. With a snap of his wrist, he turned it over. It was the king of hearts.

Leland sighed. 'Seems like I'll be getting back the gold.'

CHAPTER 6

Patrick Grady hunkered down beside his horse and examined the sprawl of hoof-prints that coated the trail, then stalked around the remnants of Jack's camp-fire. He fingered the ashes before rolling back on his haunches to peer into the hills.

'What you reckon?' Gideon asked.

Patrick stood, but then rubbed his ribs as he rose too quickly.

'Jack's group stayed here for a day or so, but they broke camp today and split. Two men headed east. The others went west.' Patrick pointed to a deeper set of tracks. 'Salvador's group have followed the main group.'

'Then we follow the main group.'

Patrick snorted. 'I got no interest in what *we* do. *I'm* heading east.'

'You're planning to pick them off a few at

a time?'

'Nope.' Patrick turned to his horse. 'Rusty has headed after those two. And I sure intend to pick him off.'

Gideon trotted his horse round to block Patrick's route.

'I can't let you do that.'

With one hand on the saddle, Patrick glared at Gideon.

'As you ain't packing a gun, you can't stop me.'

Gideon held his hands wide. 'I'm a doctor. I do no harm. And I have to do something to stop you getting yourself killed.'

'You can try. But the way I see it, you can't follow both groups.' Patrick rolled into the saddle. He sat hunched a moment, wincing, then sat tall. 'So are you stopping me killing Rusty, or following that whore?'

'Her name's Hannah,' Gideon murmured. 'And as I can't help you *and* Hannah, I have to choose which person to help, and this may not be professional, but I'll help the most decent person.' Gideon raised his eyebrows. 'And that isn't you.'

Gideon pulled on the reins and turned his horse away from Patrick. Without looking back, he headed on to the main trail and headed west, following Salvador's group.

On a flat width of rock, half-way up a canyon, Rusty lay on his belly and peered over the side at the river below. He bit his bottom lip as he aligned his sights on the two men, Fernando and Cliff, who were bustling about as they prepared to mount their horses.

For the last two hours he'd tracked these men, but when they'd stopped to water their horses at a river, he'd edged into the hills and found a good hiding-place another mile further along their route.

There, he'd waited to ambush them. But as Rusty had no experience of ambushing, other than being on the receiving end, the waiting had preyed on his nerves. So he'd doubled back and found a hidden position on the canyon side where he could look down on the river.

Now, he roved his gun towards one man, then back to the other, picking his moment. He waited until the men were mounting their horses and off balance, then fired at the rider furthest from him, Fernando.

Fernando clutched his chest and tumbled backwards from his horse.

Cliff swung into the saddle and flinched right and left as the gunshot echoed back and forth across the canyon.

Rusty blasted another shot at Cliff, but with a lithe action Cliff leapt to the side and rolled behind a boulder to disappear from sight.

Rusty kept his gun aimed at the boulder, waiting for Cliff to swing out and return fire. But long minutes passed without Cliff emerging and, with the hot sun pounding on his back, sweat erupted from Rusty's brow and the small of his back itched.

Rusty gulped and rolled to his feet. Pace by pace he edged away from the safety of his cover to gain a different angle on the canyon below.

Bent double, he glanced around. As he only saw the river, the dead man, the two horses, the fear that Cliff had doubled back up the canyon assailed Rusty and made the back of his neck itch too.

Behind him, a stone crunched against another stone.

Acting on impulse, Rusty dropped to the ground. A gunshot blasted over his tumbling form as Rusty let himself slip over the side of the canyon. He rolled twice and scrambled round to lie on his belly, facing up the slope.

He glared up at the edge of the slope, waiting for Cliff to venture an inevitable glance over the side. But again Cliff bided his time.

Rusty rolled to his feet and scrambled to his side, then up the loose scree. He rolled on to a flat length of rock and lay prone, searching for Cliff, but he saw only rocks around him and above him. For long moments he lay, then edged to his feet and paced forward.

'Who are you?' Cliff demanded.

Rusty swirled on his heel and peered in all directions, searching for Cliff's location, but saw only numerous hiding-places for his assailant.

'I'm Rusty,' he shouted, 'Rusty Anderton.'

'So,' Cliff shouted back, 'you're that man we took the gold from?'

Rusty slammed his fist against his thigh, again failing to work out from which direction Cliff's voice had come.

'Yeah. That's me.'

Cliff chuckled. 'Didn't think you'd have the guts to come after us.'

'What's that supposed to mean?'

'A yellow-belly like you should have just curled up and died.'

'I ain't no yellow-belly,' Rusty roared.

'That ain't what it looked like to me.'

Rusty hung his head a moment, gritting his teeth as he regained his composure. Then he stood tall and glanced left and right. He decided Cliff must be behind a large boulder that was standing forty yards to his right, so he raised his gun hand to the side, pointing the barrel high.

'Quit gloating and kill me, or come out

where I can see you and we can decide just who is the yellow-belly here.'

'I ain't doing that. Where's the man you shot?'

'Patrick's dead.'

'Obliged for the information. I just wanted to know why you're here before I killed you. Now you get to die.'

Cliff bobbed up from behind the nearest boulder to Rusty's left and blasted at Rusty.

Rusty threw himself to the ground, the shot cannoning feet wide. He landed flat and scrambled round to slam his elbows wide and thrust his arms into a firm triangle. He aimed his gun at arm's length and fired one shot, but already Cliff had gone to ground.

Dust flurried behind a tangle of boulders as Cliff scurried to a higher position. On his belly, Rusty kept his gun on the boulders waiting for the moment when Cliff showed himself.

A shot blasted, ploughing a dusty furrow only a foot to Rusty's side.

Rusty narrowed his eyes as he stared up at

the rocks searching for Cliff who just had to be hiding there. But he saw only rocks.

In irritation, he fired a speculative shot. Then a high shot blasted over his head. Rusty heard the lead ricochet off the rocks ahead and he winced as he realized the shooter was behind him. He rolled on to his back and searched for this new assailant, but another high shot blasted into the rocks thirty yards above him and he realized this man wasn't aiming at him.

Another shot ripped out and this time Rusty saw a flash of colour as Cliff staggered out from his cover and tumbled over a rock.

Seconds later a loud thud of a body falling on hard ground forced Rusty to hang his head for a moment.

Then Rusty jumped to his feet and dashed to the rocks to see the body roll to a halt twenty yards from him and sprawl on to his back.

'Who did that?' Rusty shouted, swirling round on the spot.

Rusty's cry echoed down the canyon. He

turned and repeated his demand, but then fifty yards away, Patrick Grady stepped out from behind a boulder.

'You did well in getting one of them,' Patrick shouted. He levelled his gun at Rusty's head. 'But that's your last success.'

CHAPTER 7

With Patrick having left Gideon to pursue Salvador on his own, Gideon could no longer ignore his reasons for his journey. He hurried to a gallop.

Within an hour, he caught his first sight of Salvador, riding ahead at a mile-eating trot.

Gideon took a deep breath and hailed one of the backing riders. He waited for a returning hail, then galloped on to meet the group.

The riders drew to a halt and formed a semicircle with Salvador setting his horse forward from the rest.

Gideon drew his horse to a halt before them. He glanced at Hannah, who stared back with no hint of her usual good humour. Then he faced Salvador.

'What do you want?' Salvador grunted.

Gideon took a deep breath. 'Figured that I was right when you first told me you were going after Jack – someone has to be around to fill the bullet holes and bury the bodies.'

Salvador narrowed his eyes as he appraised Gideon.

'That ain't the real reason.'

'It's part of the reason.' Gideon hung his head, then shrugged. 'What with all that gold around, I figured I might get something for providing you with some doctoring.'

'Hey,' Zane Singer whined, 'we got all the help we need. We ain't cutting him in.'

'We ain't,' Salvador said. He rubbed his chin, then leaned forward in the saddle. 'But perhaps Gideon's right. Some doctorin' might be called for. And we might be prepared to pay for it.'

'I ain't accepting that,' Zane muttered.

'Be quiet, or you'll be Gideon's first patient.'

Zane glared back a moment, then glanced around the semicircle of men, but as nobody met his gaze, he set his jaw firm and stared straight ahead.

For long moments Salvador glared at Zane, then turned back to Gideon.

'You can come with us,' he said. 'But if I reckon you got some other plan in mind...' Salvador raised his eyebrows and grinned.

Gideon held his hands wide. 'Like what? I don't pack a gun.'

Salvador shrugged. 'I dunno. But the same rules apply to you as apply to Hannah. Keep quiet. Do as I tell you to. And give me no reason to think you're plannin' anythin'.'

Salvador waved a finger above his head in a circular motion and the riders disbanded to form into their previous line, with four men staying back and five men scouting ahead.

Gideon edged into the middle of the group to ride alongside Hannah. He glanced at her, but she continued to face the front and ride silently. But when the riders had hurried to their former trot and edged a distance apart, she looked at him.

'Why have you followed us?' she said, her voice low.

Gideon coughed. 'I reckon you know.'

'I don't.' She flashed him a harsh smile. 'It can't be anything to do with me, because you know I can take care of myself a whole lot better than you can take care of yourself.'

'Yeah,' Gideon snapped. 'Like you said, it can't be anything to do with you.'

This time, Gideon turned to face the front and although his cheeks tingled as if Hannah continued to look at him, he resisted all temptation to turn to her.

'Patrick,' Rusty said, shaking his head, 'a man in your condition should be resting.'

Patrick grunted a laugh and stalked towards Rusty. When he was ten yards away, he stood sideways and firmed his gun hand, his gaze resolute.

'Seems I ain't.'

'I know.' Rusty pointed at the body lying sprawled beside him. 'You did well. That man was all set to kill me.'

'I ain't looking for thanks.' Patrick grinned. 'I was just saving you so I could kill myself.'

'I don't reckon that's you talking.' Rusty edged a pace to the side and pointed at Cliff's body. 'And as I reckon that man had left Jack's group, we might have got some of our gold back already.'

Patrick snorted and raised his gun hand a mite.

'*We* ain't done anything.'

Rusty hung his head a moment, then looked up and held his arms wide.

'Patrick, you ain't still thinking that I shot you, are you?'

'I sure am.' Patrick rubbed his left hand over the bandages encasing his chest. 'You never forget your partner blasting lead in your guts.'

'I didn't shoot you. I told you.' Moving

with extreme slowness, Rusty unhooked his gunbelt and held it to his side, then stared at Patrick, his eyes wide and pleading. 'And I know you, Patrick. You won't kill an unarmed man, whatever you suspect he did.'

Rusty rolled the belt over one shoulder, then sauntered to Cliff's side. He toed the body over and rummaged through his clothing. He frowned, then stood back.

'Rusty,' Patrick muttered, 'stop ignoring me.'

Rusty kept his gaze away from Patrick as he stood and walked to the edge of the canyon. On the edge he stood a moment, then paced over the side.

Patrick jumped on the spot, then scurried to the canyon side and peered down.

'Stop!' Patrick shouted, but Rusty was already sliding on his heels down the canyon side.

Patrick aimed his gun at Rusty's receding back, then snorted and hurried to follow him.

In a huge cloud of dust both men slithered

to the bottom, Patrick ten yards behind Rusty.

At the bottom, Rusty still kept his gaze away from Patrick and dashed to the second body. He rummaged through Fernando's clothing, then checked on the dead men's horses. A low whistle escaped his lips. He turned to Patrick, smiling, and pointed at the bags dangling from Cliff's saddle.

'They do have a share of the gold. Seems we–'

'Quit ignoring me!' Patrick shouted. He aimed his gun at Rusty's head. 'You're a man who tried to kill me and you'll face that now.'

'Patrick, you're a good man. You'd never kill someone based on a suspicion that he might have tried to kill you.'

Patrick's gun hand shook, but he grabbed it with his other hand, stopping the shaking.

'You're right. I wouldn't kill based on a suspicion. But I don't have a suspicion. I know what I saw. And I saw your gun fire and I felt lead rip into my guts. That's all the proof I'll ever need.'

As Patrick advanced a long pace, Rusty dropped his gunbelt at his feet and raised his hands to shoulder level, then spread his arms wide. With his gaze set firmly on Patrick, he puffed his chest and jutted his chin.

'Then don't just stand there telling me what you want to do, shoot me and make us even, because we have the rest of our gold to get back and arguing is just slowing us down.'

Patrick looked Rusty up and down, then set his feet wide and nodded.

'All right. Tell me what happened. As you're my former partner, I'll trust anything you say.'

'Obliged.'

'Don't thank me. If I let you live and I ever find out that you've lied to me, I'll track you down and kill you.' Patrick firmed his gun arm. 'So tell me. What happened in Hangman's Gulch?'

Rusty took a deep breath and centred his gaze on a spot two feet above Patrick's head.

'One of Jack's gang shot you. He must have guessed–'

'Liar! You shot me. I saw the gunsmoke.'

'That's because I fired my only bullet. But I didn't fire it at you.'

Patrick snorted. 'And after you fired at someone else, you don't expect me to believe that Jack let you go, do you?'

Rusty swung his right arm in until the hand was pointing at Patrick. The hand was shaking with an uncontrollable tremor.

'You know I ain't brave like you. I was scared and my hand was shaking even worse than it is now. My aim was so poor nobody realized I'd fired at anyone but you.'

'Jack Wolf is the leader of the worst gang of bandits around. He wouldn't just let you go.'

'Jack may be a bandit, but he honours his promises. The cards said one of us would go free if we fought a showdown, and as we did – sort of – he let me go.'

Patrick locked his arm and narrowed his eyes.

'I don't believe a word of that.' Patrick glared at Rusty, but as Rusty still couldn't meet his gaze, he snorted. 'You're lying. I can see it in your eyes.'

Rusty lowered his head and scuffed the earth at his feet. He gulped with a pronounced sound, then looked straight at Patrick.

'You're right,' he whispered, his voice as light as the wind. 'I was lying. I shot you.'

Patrick closed his eyes a moment.

'I wanted to hear the words, but now you've said them, I hardly believe it.'

'But it ain't like it sounds.'

'Then what is it?'

Rusty stumbled back, then slumped to the ground and sat. With his lips pursed, hc hugged his knees and rocked back and forth. Then he stopped the rocking and looked up, his eyes brimming with tears.

'Take that gun off me and I'll tell you.'

Patrick held his gun on Rusty a moment longer, then lowered his arm to his side.

'Go on.'

'I was doing like you said,' Rusty said, his voice faint. 'I picked one of Jack's men to shoot at. He was standing behind you and I reckoned he'd shoot you in the back when he realized we were fighting back. So when you went for your gun, I shot at him, but I was shaking and my aim was all wild, and I...'

Rusty snuffled and rubbed a shaking hand over his face.

'You mean you hit me by accident?'

Rusty nodded. He scuffed at his eyes, wiping away moisture.

'Yup.'

Patrick rubbed his chin. 'But you said it wasn't you straight away. You lied even then.'

Rusty slammed the flat of his hand against his brow.

'I reckoned you'd die and I didn't want your last sight to be me killing you.' He lowered his voice to a whisper. 'So I panicked and lied.'

'And afterwards? Why did Jack let you live?'

'With you half-dead, I told Jack that I won the showdown. He believed me. He even gave me a few dollars for the entertainment before everyone left. I got you to Destitution and you know the rest.'

Patrick snorted his disbelief and aimed his gun straight at Rusty's chest, but his arm shook with an involuntary tremor. He planted his feet wide and gritted his teeth, but no matter how hard he gripped his gun, the shaking just worsened until, inch by inch, he lowered his arm.

'Damn you, Rusty,' he muttered, slamming a fist against his thigh. 'I know what I saw you do and that was no accident. But I can't shoot you in cold blood. I ain't anything like–'

A gunshot blasted, ripping shards from a rock ten yards to Patrick's side. He darted a glance over his shoulder.

Two riders, Leland and Tort, were hurtling down the canyon and straight for them, their guns thrust out and blasting at them.

CHAPTER 8

At the brow of a rounded hill, Salvador Milano halted the line of horses. Below, a long river wended a snaking path to the north, but on a jutting headland stood the abandoned compound of Fort Clemency.

The French had originally built this fort, but recently the cavalry had abandoned it too and now it was rapidly falling into disrepair. The stockade of logs still stood, but the buildings inside were now crumbling.

In case Jack had stopped there for the night, Salvador turned and encouraged the other riders to back so that they didn't present an obvious outline against the sky.

When everyone had retreated, Salvador gestured back to Hannah for her to approach him.

Hannah darted a glance at Gideon, but as

he was still staring straight ahead, she paced her horse forward. When she drew alongside, Salvador raised his eyebrows.

'Well,' he said, 'd'you reckon Jack might stop there?'

Hannah shrugged. 'I don't know Jack that well, but he'll have to stop for the night somewhere, and that fort seems safe.'

'I didn't ask what you reckoned,' Salvador snapped. 'You're here for one reason – you know Jack. So would he stop there?'

Hannah sneered. 'As I'm here for just one reason, perhaps I should head down to the fort and find out.'

'Now you're gettin' the right idea.' Salvador widened his eyes. 'You know what to do, don't you?'

Hannah fluffed her hair, a sly smile emerging.

'From what the girls said about you, I don't reckon you can teach me anything.'

Mack Hoffer gibbered his amusement, but Salvador cut him off with a harsh glare, then swirled back to Hannah, his eyes blazing.

'Watch what you're sayin' or when we take Jack, the lesson you'll learn will be your last.' Salvador glared at Hannah a moment longer.

Hannah met Salvador's gaze, but still a small gulp escaped.

'I know what I have to do. I've remembered the signal.'

Salvador edged his horse to her side and lowered his voice.

'Good. Don't try anythin' and this'll end right fine for all of us.' Salvador swirled round and nodded to Mack. 'And as you were mighty amused by this, you're going with her to check she ain't minded to try anythin'.'

'Hey,' Mack whined. 'They'll be alone. How will I know what she says to Jack?'

'You won't.' Salvador chuckled and glanced around the arc of men. 'But don't go worryin' 'bout us. If you don't give the signal, we ain't riskin' our lives.'

Mack glanced at Rodrigo, then Olen, then the other men, searching for support, but he received nothing but blank glares. With much grumbling, Mack pulled his horse to the side and drew alongside Hannah.

'What you so nervous about?' Hannah asked, a grim smile on her lips.

Mack gulped and raised the reins in a shaking hand.

'I reckon I'm dead no matter what happens. If you double-cross us, Jack kills me. If you don't, the second I give the signal, I get to die first.'

Hannah glanced at Mack. 'If you carry on shaking like that, you'll be dead long before I even get to thinking about double-crossing you. Come on.'

Hannah rode ahead a pace, the reluctant and slow Mack at her heels, but Gideon raised a hand.

'Wait!' he shouted.

Hannah and Mack halted and glanced over their shoulders.

'For what?' Salvador said.

Gideon rode up to face Salvador. 'Mack doesn't need to go into the fort with Hannah.

I'll go in with her instead.'

'Best idea I've heard,' Mack said. He whooped and cantered back to the main group.

'You ain't goin' into the fort,' Salvador muttered, shaking his head.

'Why?'

'I ain't got to give you no reason, but bein' as you asked so nicely – Jack ain't seen Mack, but he'll smell trouble the moment he sees your ugly hide again.'

'He hasn't seen me before. He was only in Destitution for a night and spent most of his time with Hannah. The rest of the time he was tormenting you.'

Salvador glanced away a moment, then turned his gaze on Gideon and leaned forward in the saddle.

'Ain't convincing me. Mack goes with her.'

With a steady gaze, Gideon glanced around the ragbag bunch that had accompanied Salvador on this foolhardy mission, then snorted.

'You obviously haven't looked at your followers properly. If any of them rode into that fort, Jack would know something was wrong.' Gideon held his hands wide and put on his best smile. 'But I don't look like trouble.'

Salvador followed Gideon's slow gaze around the group, appraising his motley collection of lowlifes. He matched Gideon's snort.

'I guess you ain't lookin' like trouble.' Salvador lowered his head a moment. 'All right. You can go with Hannah. But make sure she doesn't do anythin', or you'll see the sort of hell we can raise.'

Gideon tipped his hat and rode from the group, but he trotted past Hannah without looking at her. He trotted over the brow of the hill and kept his gaze set forward so that Hannah had to speed to a gallop to join him.

She edged ahead a pace and glanced back at him.

'Suppose you reckon I should thank you

for coming with me,' she said.

'Not saying that,' Gideon murmured with his jaw set firm.

'Good.' Hannah set her gaze forward. 'Because I ain't.'

Beside the river, Patrick and Rusty shared a glance. Then Patrick dashed for the cover of a tangle of rocks fifty yards to his right.

Rusty rolled to the side and grabbed his gunbelt from the ground, then hurtled after Patrick as he slipped it round his waist.

At a gallop Leland and Tort bore down on them, their guns blasting with every stride.

One gunshot gouged into the earth scant inches from Rusty's right boot, another ripped through his hat.

Rusty thrust his head down and wheeled his arms as he fought for more speed. With each pace, he gained on Patrick, until Patrick hurtled behind a boulder. Rusty threw up his hands and in a long rolling dive tumbled behind it to crash into Patrick.

Patrick shrugged away from Rusty,

clutching his ribs.

'You hurt?' Rusty asked as he rolled to a kneeling position.

'Nope. Just trying to be careful like the doctor told me to. You banging into me like that ain't helping.'

Rusty glanced over the boulder to see the two assailants dismount and dash behind another boulder twenty yards before them. He ducked and leaned against the boulder beside Patrick.

He noted Patrick's pale complexion, the beads of sweat on his brow, his slumped posture, his heavy breathing.

'You don't look well, Patrick.'

Patrick wheezed, then cleared his throat and sat up straight, wincing with the effort.

'I been hearing that a lot since you shot me.'

'I didn't shoot...' Rusty lowered his head a moment and sighed. 'Stay here and cover me. I'll get them.'

'Sure.' Patrick sneered at Rusty. 'You can trust me.'

Rusty glared at Patrick, then bobbed up. As neither of their assailants was visible, he jumped to his feet and dashed at an angle to their covering boulder.

He'd dashed ten paces when Tort bobbed up and fired at him. Rusty hurled himself to the ground, rolling over his right shoulder as lead whistled by his tumbling form. He continued the roll and flopped to a halt on his belly, aiming towards the rock.

For long moments he waited for someone to venture out. Then Tort leapt up. In an instant Rusty fired and this time Tort fell back, his hands clawing at his chest. Rusty didn't wait to see whether his gunfire had been as deadly as he hoped and charged at the rock.

In five long strides he reached the rock and threw himself over it. Leland was crouched on the other side and with a great clawing swipe, Rusty grabbed him round the neck and tumbled him to the ground. Both men rolled over and over, each trying to pin the other down.

'Patrick, help,' Rusty shouted. 'I got–'

Leland clawed up. He clutched Rusty around the neck and dragged him down. Then, using his greater weight, he rolled Rusty on his back.

In desperation, Rusty bucked and tried to knock Leland to the side, but Leland bore down with all his weight on Rusty's chest. Rusty glanced to his side and from the corner of his eye, he saw Patrick poke his head up from behind the boulder and fire, but his shot whistled over Leland's head.

Leland still flinched and, using this momentary advantage, Rusty bucked Leland away. But Leland grabbed a firm grip around Rusty's neck and both men tumbled to the side, then staggered to their feet, each holding the other in a bear hug.

'Shoot him,' Rusty screeched.

'You're too close,' Patrick shouted, pacing out from behind his cover.

Leland glanced to the side at Patrick, then pulled Rusty round so he was between him and Patrick. With a short-arm jab, he slugged

Rusty's jaw, knocking him back. Even before Rusty hit the ground, he was dashing towards the riverbank.

Standing sideways, Patrick blasted a shot at him. It was wild but Leland skidded to a halt, dropped to one knee, and blasted lead at Patrick.

Patrick hurled himself behind his covering rock but as Leland ripped another wild shot at Patrick's tumbling form, Rusty ran and dived at Leland, bundling him back and over the side of the riverbank.

Both men floundered as they searched for purchase on the slippery ground, but Rusty was the first to gain his footing and with a long round-armed slug to the jaw, rocked Leland back a pace.

Leland flailed his arms, searching for balance, but then tottered to the side to land heavily and in an avalanche of stone and dirt tumbled head over heels into the river with a great splash.

Rusty sat. For long moments he trained his gun on the water, but when Leland bobbed back up, he was floating face down, his arms wide and still.

Still, Rusty watched the body swirl downstream until it drifted beyond a large tangle of fallen trees. Then he jumped to his feet and climbed over the riverbank to face Patrick. He smiled.

'Seems we fought well when we were a team again.'

Patrick glared back a moment, then nodded and produced a thin smile while rubbing his ribs.

'Suppose we did,' he murmured.

'But more important that that – you made a good decision before they arrived.' Rusty lowered his voice. 'We should be friends.'

'We should.' Patrick sighed and tipped back his hat with his gun barrel. 'But I don't know if I can trust you again.'

Rusty shuffled to Patrick's side with his head down.

'Don't worry about that now. When we have our gold back, you can decide what you want to do.' Rusty gestured down at Tort's body and forced a thin smile. 'Like I was trying to tell you before, these men have got their share of our gold-dust on them, so we've got some of it back already.'

For long moments Patrick stared at Rusty, then glanced at Tort's body. He snorted and holstered his gun as he stalked to Tort's horse. He unhooked one of the bags of gold dust. In his right hand he hefted the bag, then turned to face Rusty and forced a smile.

'Come on,' he said. 'We got the rest of our gold to get back.'

CHAPTER 9

One hundred yards from Fort Clemency, the mixture of anger and fear that had persuaded Gideon to accompany Hannah faded from his mind and he pulled back on the reins, slowing his horse to walking pace.

'I'll do the talking,' he shouted after Hannah.

Hannah pulled her horse to a halt and stood sideways across the trail.

'Why?' she muttered.

Gideon swung his horse around her and continued down the hill.

'Because I have to.'

Hannah hurried on to ride beside him and glared at Gideon.

'Why won't you look at me and tell me what you're doing here?'

For long moments Gideon rode in silence, but fifty yards from the fort, he saw someone bob up from behind the stockade. He coughed and jutted his chin.

'I don't have to explain myself. I just want us both to get out of this alive and I reckon if I do the talking, I can do that.'

Hannah sighed. 'You still reckon that you can help me better than I can help myself. Well, you're wrong. I can take care of myself.'

'I'm sure you can. It's just...'

Hannah glanced at the fort. There, the

wooden gate swung open and two men edged through. As they raised their rifles and aimed one at each of them, she gulped.

'But I suppose I shouldn't complain if my brother has my best interests at heart.'

'Brother?'

'Yeah,' Hannah said. 'If you want to live, you're my brother. And I'll do the talking.'

Gideon glanced at Hannah and opened his mouth to argue, but ahead the two men stalked out from the fort and firmed their gun arms.

'Then that's who I am, sister,' he murmured, then hunched forward in the saddle.

The two men paced into the centre of the trail and beckoned for Gideon and Hannah to halt twenty yards from them.

The man on the left, Strang Chase, edged forward a pace.

'What do you want?' he muttered.

Hannah held her chin aloft.

'I want to see Jack,' she said. As Strang snorted, she smiled. 'I followed his tracks.'

Strang glanced at the other man, Armstrong Stacker, who sneered.

'That's a mighty clever talent for such a scrawny girl.'

'I have many talents, as Jack knows.' Hannah tapped her chin as she appraised Armstrong. 'And I recognize you from the Belle Starr.'

Armstrong lowered his hat a mite and narrowed his eyes.

'And now I come to think about it, I recognize you.' He whistled through his teeth. 'You're a saloon-girl and you're all the way out here.'

Hannah fluffed her hair and fluttered her eyelashes.

'I'm not just any saloon-girl. I'm a saloon-girl who caught Jack's eye. And I don't reckon he'll appreciate you keeping me from him.'

Armstrong gulped. 'Guess as you're right.'

Armstrong and Strang backed to the side of the trail and held their arms to the side, directing her into the fort, but then Strang's head snapped to the side to glare at Gideon.

'You can come in,' he muttered. 'He can't.'

Hannah slammed her hands on her hips. 'He can't just hang around outside. And I intend to be here a while.' She shrugged. 'And he's harmless. He's a doctor. He doesn't even pack a gun.'

From under his low hat, Armstrong glared at Gideon a while longer, appraising his apparent unarmed status.

Gideon forced his lips into his most benign smile.

Slowly, Armstrong and Strang nodded and with their suspicious glares burning into Gideon's back, Gideon and Hannah rode into the fort.

Strang trotted after them. He beckoned them to the side of the gate and watched them dismount. He still frisked them both, taking longer with Hannah than with Gideon. With a few barked commands, he ordered Don Ritter to lead their horses to the stable, then ordered Armstrong to watch Gideon while he took Hannah to see Jack.

Hannah flashed Gideon a smile. Gideon

tried to return one, but his face froze and he could only stare at her.

She turned, and he watched Strang lead her across the fort's wide parade ground and into a substantial stone building to the side – the powder magazine.

Hannah strode into the magazine behind Strang, her skirts swinging, but she didn't look Gideon's way.

Gideon hung his head and glanced at Armstrong. As Armstrong just leaned against the gate, Gideon blew out his cheeks and held his hands behind his back. He couldn't stop himself crossing his fingers.

Once she was inside the powder magazine, Hannah glanced around, blinking frequently as her eyes became accustomed to the gloom.

She appraised the stark, windowless building quickly. The blastproof walls were four feet thick. The door she stood before was the only entrance. Across the centre of the building was a wooden wall. The doorway to the second room opened on to the main storage area and, although she was sure that no powder would still be here, in the darkness a pile of bags nestled against the back wall.

Hannah tore her gaze from her appraisal of the room and smiled at Jack who was sitting, leaning against the side wall. He looked at Hannah with his one eye, but it was blank and secretive.

'What you doing here?' he said, his voice flat.

Hannah set her hands on her hips and held a leg to the side, arching a trim calf.

'That's a mighty fine greeting for your favourite saloon-girl.'

'That's as maybe, but my question stands.' Jack rolled to his feet and stalked a pace towards her. 'What you doing here?'

Hannah grinned. 'I came to see you.'

For long moments Jack glared at her, his single eye still cold. He glanced at Strang, who shrugged.

'And how did you find me?'

'She and this other man tracked us,' Strang said. 'If you believe her.'

Jack flashed Strang a harsh glare.

'I'll decide what I believe. Leave us.' He glared at Strang until he sauntered from the room, then turned to Hannah. 'Why are you really here?'

Hannah shrugged, then took a deep breath. 'I had to know.'

'Had to know what?'

'You're the only man who's ever treated me right. I got to find out why that is.'

'And if the answer means we can never amount to anything?'

'I'll leave and you'll never see me again.'

Jack walked in a circle, throwing out his legs with a slight swagger as he paced. When he'd completed a full circle, he faced off to Hannah.

'And who is the man with you?'

'My brother, Gideon.'

Jack's upper lip snarled. 'And your brother just happened to ride with you when you discovered I have gold?'

'It ain't like that. He arrived just after you left Destitution. I'd been writing home, claiming I was fine and that I had regular work and money for lodgings.' Hannah glanced away. 'But when he discovered what I was doing, he told me to go home with him.'

'You wouldn't follow a man's orders.'

'I didn't. I decided to go home with him. But before I left, I had to hear what you had to say.'

Jack nodded, his hand straying up to brush his top pocket.

'You know that.'

'I don't.'

Jack smiled and extracted the pack of cards from his top pocket. He held them out.

'Present your options, then ask the cards.'

Hannah glared at the cards, then shook her head.

'No. I want to know what you want, not what a random card says.'

'If you want to know me,' Jack said, turning the pack over in his hand, 'you'll take a card.'

Jack thrust the cards out, then fanned them.

'All right.' Hannah took a deep breath. 'A non-face card says I stay with you. A two-eyed card says I leave. Are those good choices?'

'Yup. The most likely card has to be what you want to do.'

'If it's a one-eyed card...' Hannah glanced away.

'Go on. The one-eyed card has to be the unthinkable.'

Hannah nodded, then turned back to meet Jack's gaze.

'A one-eyed card says you'll kill me.'

Jack grinned, his one eye bright. 'You understand. Now, ask the cards what you have to do.'

Hannah reached for the pack. With her hand shaking with the slightest of tremors, she withdrew a card.

With the card lying flat on her palm, she stared at the card's back, trying to anticipate her fate before she saw it.

Then she closed her eyes and swung the card over. She cracked her eyes open and glanced at the card, then, sighing deeply, looked up at Jack.

Jack was staring deep into her eyes.

'And?' he whispered.

'Two of spades,' she said.

'I know.' He smiled. 'You were fated to stay.'

CHAPTER 10

When Strang emerged from the powder magazine, he took Armstrong aside and grunted a few words to him. Then Armstrong led Gideon to the stable, which was opposite the gate. On the ground before the stable, Jack's men had set out a row of blankets.

Gideon laid out his own blanket, but with that task complete, Armstrong left him to do as he pleased. None of Jack's other men paid him anything but the most cursory attention.

From the few muttered comments he did receive, Gideon decided that everyone had accepted he was Hannah's brother. And, as Gideon didn't want to risk saying something that might disagree with any story Hannah was telling Jack, he didn't dare initiate any conversation. So instead, he occupied his time by sauntering around the fort.

The compound was in a sorry state of disrepair. Only two buildings were complete and sturdy: the powder magazine at the side of the parade ground and the officers' quarters beside the gate. These buildings were both stone. The ramshackle stable still stood, but only because the back wall was the stockade and it supported the structure.

The collapsed remains of at least three other timber buildings were dotted around the parade ground, but whether they'd collapsed from lack of use or from the fort's activities, Gideon couldn't tell for sure. But as the wooden stockade around the complex and the raised look-out platform five feet from the top were just about continuous, Gideon guessed that the fort was in use right up until it had been abandoned.

At the back of the powder magazine, a ten-foot length of the stockade had collapsed. Through it, he saw earthworks consisting of a ditch and raised earth, which provided defence on the non-river side of the fort. The forest was beyond. Aside from the gate, this appeared to be the only way in and out of the fort.

Two of Jack's men steadily patrolled the raised platform. They stopped to chat and glance outside over the occasional shortened logs but their patrol traced a route that frequently passed the collapsed length of stockade. From this observation, Gideon reckoned that Jack believed this was the fort's greatest weakness.

As he didn't want to draw too much attention to his interest in the fort's surroundings and the guards' procedures, Gideon returned to sit in the parade ground and watch the other men bustle around him.

He saw no sign of the gold that these men had stolen from Patrick and Rusty, but from the men's calmness, Gideon guessed it was well hidden.

At sundown, Brady lit a fire and cooked a thin stew.

With his cooking completed, Hannah and Jack emerged from the powder magazine to eat it.

Gideon tried to catch Hannah's eye, but she pointedly sat away from him and kept her gaze on either her food or Jack. As soon as Jack finished eating, he barked commands to Strang, who in turn barked them to the others, then retired to the powder magazine with Hannah.

Then the men just chatted in small groups, again making no effort to drag Gideon into their confidence. As Gideon still hadn't been able to talk to Hannah, he was content with their indifference.

Around two hours after sundown most of the men retired to sleep. Within minutes, their rasping snores filled the parade ground.

But as during the day, two men stayed awake to patrol the raised look-out platform and parade ground.

Under his solitary blanket Gideon lay back and through narrowed eyes, followed the guards' routine, ensuring that it was identical to their routine during daylight hours.

After two hours, the guards changed, but by this time Gideon was confident that he knew their patrolling routine and decided to make his move. He watched a guard saunter across the parade ground and listened to his footfalls recede behind the tumbledown stable, then rolled from his blanket and stood – he had twenty minutes to leave the fort, see Salvador, then return.

It was four hours into the night and the moon was yet to rise. Only the fading remnants of a camp-fire lit the parade ground in subdued, shadow-filled light.

He edged along the stable wall to reach the powder magazine. He listened for any sounds emerging from within, but on hearing nothing but the wind, he tiptoed to the back of the powder magazine and climbed over the fallen logs that littered the gap in the fence.

Once outside, he hurried to a trot and within a minute he was over the earthworks and into the trees, and within another minute the fort had disappeared into the gloom behind him.

For the first one hundred yards he kept back from the trail, making slow progress through the thick forest, but when he crested the hill in front of the fort, he headed back to the trail. Once there, he broke into a run and dashed down the slope to enter Salvador's camp.

All of Salvador's men were snoring. Only Zane Singer was on guard, but he was sitting, leaning against a rock and snoring even louder than the others were.

Gideon stood over him, tapping a foot on the ground and when even this failed to rouse him, he shook his shoulder.

Zane flinched, his right hand scrambling for his gun, but then he squinted at Gideon.

'That you, Gideon?'

'Yup.'

Zane snorted and raised his hand. 'Then don't sneak up on me like that again.'

'How else am I supposed to get out of the fort other than to sneak?'

Zane shrugged and with a huge yawn and a stretch, he led him into the campsite.

Gideon stood beside the dying remnants of their low fire while Zane shook Salvador awake.

Salvador yawned and clapped his mouth open and closed, then sneered when he saw Gideon.

'Why are you here?' he muttered, rolling to his feet.

'To tell you what I've learnt.'

'We agreed on your signal. You don't need to be here.'

'And as I want to come out of this alive, I reckoned giving you some more inform-ation might be useful.'

Salvador glared back a moment, then nodded.

'What you got?'

Gideon grabbed a twig from beside the fire. On the ground, he traced the pattern of the buildings that he'd seen inside the fort. He placed crosses in the parade ground to signify the location of most of the men, a large cross for Jack's location in the powder magazine, and a line for the route he'd taken to leave the fort.

Salvador nodded. 'Good information. Are they asleep?'

'Most are. Two are on guard, but they leave gaps in their routine. That's how I got out.'

Salvador slammed his fist into an open palm.

'Then we take Jack.'

Gideon shook his head. 'Not yet.'

'Why?' Salvador grunted.

'Because I want your attack to work. I've told you the layout so you can plan a proper assault.'

Salvador snorted and slapped Gideon's shoulder, knocking him back a pace.

'You tryin' to say I ain't got the courage to

take on Jack?'

'No,' Gideon murmured, rubbing his shoulder. 'I'm just saying that I'll find out more about his arrangements and pick the right moment for you to take him.'

'I make the decisions.'

'You do. But if you take my advice, you'll get the gold.' Gideon smiled. 'And look at it this way: Jack is staying there, so you have time to wait and pick your moment.'

Salvador rubbed his chin as he glanced away, then turned back and provided a begrudging nod.

'I'll wait,' he murmured.

'Obliged.' Gideon tipped his hat and turned.

'But I ain't waitin' for long. I want that gold.'

Gideon opened his mouth to argue, but then shrugged and with a last nod to Salvador, he dashed from the site and back towards the fort.

He guessed that he'd already used nearly twenty minutes and within a few more minutes, one of the guards would patrol past his blanket in the parade ground. He also guessed that being away for one passage wouldn't alarm the guards, but being away a second time would.

He reached as near to the fort as he dared along the trail, then headed into the trees. In the thick undergrowth, he made slow progress. He reckoned that the rapidly diminishing available time was causing his heart to hammer loud enough to alert the guards. And in his haste, he tripped over every tangle of root and walked into every dangling branch.

Long, long minutes had passed and he was sure he must have passed his first twenty minutes period when the black outline of the fort loomed against the night sky.

Gideon sighed his relief and stopped a moment to rest a hand on his chest. He took several deep breaths while he gazed along the top of the stockade, ensuring the guards weren't on this side, then set off again.

A hand clamped on his shoulder.

Gideon flinched. A strangulated cry emerged from his lips, but he still reached back and grabbed the arm, then dropped to his knees. He yanked on the arm, trying to throw his assailant over his shoulder, but a second firm arm wrapped itself over his mouth and pulled him straight.

'Be quiet,' a voice whispered beside his ear.

Gideon struggled a moment, then relaxed as he recognized Patrick's voice. He nodded and Patrick released his grip.

'What you doing here?' Gideon whispered.

Patrick shuffled round to kneel beside Gideon.

'Trying to get into the fort. And as you got out, I reckon you can help me there.'

Gideon sighed. 'Suppose you being here means you've already sorted out your other problem?'

Patrick sneered and glanced over his shoulder.

Another man stepped out from behind a

tree. Even in the faint starlight, Gideon recognized Rusty.

'Not totally,' Rusty said.

'You're partners again?'

Rusty glanced at Patrick, who snorted.

'Nope,' Patrick said, 'we're just heading in the same direction.'

'Well, at least you've resolved your differences without one of you killing the other.'

Rusty shrugged, but Patrick kneaded his brow.

'At least that,' he muttered.

Gideon pointed to the fort, then rolled to his feet.

'And I have to go before somebody misses me.'

Patrick jumped to his feet and paced round to stand before Gideon.

'You have enough time to tell us what you've learnt.'

'I haven't got...' Gideon wavered a moment. Time was pressing heavily on him, but he judged that arguing with someone as bull-headed as Patrick was doomed to fail, so he quickly ran through the layout of the fort and what he knew about Jack's arrangements inside.

'And you wait for my signal,' he said, ending his explanation.

Rusty nodded, but Patrick shook his head.

'I'm guessing you just told that to Salvador too.'

Gideon bit his bottom lip to suppress a wince.

'I did.'

'So you got to answer my question – whose side are you on?'

'Nobody's. I'm only here to get Hannah out safely when Salvador attacks Jack. I don't care who gets the gold.'

'That ain't no answer,' Patrick snapped. 'You're either on my side or you ain't.'

'I'm not taking anyone's side but my own. I'll just give the signal to Salvador to attack when I reckon it's the best time to get Hannah out. What you decide to do then and what Salvador decides to do, isn't my concern.'

As Patrick glanced away, muttering to himself, Rusty nodded.

'I reckon we can't ask for anything more,' he said.

Gideon patted Rusty's and Patrick's backs.

'And I have to get back in before anybody realizes I'm missing and this discussion becomes irrelevant.'

Rusty held his hands high. 'Go on. We'll just wait for the signal.'

'We won't,' Patrick muttered and squared off to Rusty.

But as the two men settled into a muttered argument, Gideon backed away from them, then broke into a run and headed towards the fort.

Despite being away for over forty minutes, Gideon slipped back into the fort without any problems. The guards were out of sight, and he was able to wander straight into the parade ground and to his blanket.

For the rest of the night, his multitude of worries caused him to slip fitfully in and out of sleep. But to his surprise, it was still dark when he heard Hannah shuffle into a blanket two yards to his left.

Gideon waited until the grumbled mutterings from the other men about this interruption drifted to snoring, then he slipped along the ground to her side.

'You fine?' he whispered.

Hannah nodded. She lay on her back, staring at the night sky.

'Yeah.'

'Jack had enough of you?'

'He likes to be alone when he has an important decision to make.'

'Reckoned he'd want as much of your company as he could get.'

'It ain't like that.' For the first time she turned her head to look at Gideon. In the faint moonlight moisture gleamed in her eyes as she lowered her voice to the lowest of whispers. 'He doesn't touch me.'

Gideon gulped. 'You mean...'

'Yeah. He's the only man who wants to be with me, but doesn't want to grope and paw me.' She considered Gideon a moment, then flashed him a smile. 'Aside from you.'

'But he paid for you in Destitution.'

'He did.' Hannah rolled on her back to look at the sky. 'But he prefers to talk.'

'Why?'

'I don't know,' she snapped, then rubbed the back of her hand over her nose and snuffled. 'But I want to find out.'

'Why? Jack is an ugly, one-eyed varmint.'

Hannah rubbed her angular cheeks, her eyes downcast. 'Looks ain't everything.'

'But you're a mighty fine-looking...' Gideon sighed and took a long, deep breath. 'Just don't waste your time on him. Jack is a killer.'

Hannah drew her blanket to her chin. 'He has no qualms about hurting other people, but he's gentle with me.'

'That doesn't sound like the notorious bandit Jack Wolf to me.'

'It doesn't, and that's why I want to know why a man who is so sure of himself lets the random turn of a card govern him.' She shrugged the blanket even higher and rolled on to her side, her legs tucked up. 'He's a fascinating man.'

She stared at Gideon, then slowly closed her eyes.

Gideon watched her drift into sleep, then rolled on to his back. 'That's one word for him,' he whispered.

CHAPTER 11

Throughout the remainder of the night, Patrick and Rusty took turns to watch the fort and follow the guards' movements as they patrolled the raised lookout platform.

But for the last hours before sun-up Rusty was asleep and left Patrick to his brooding vigil.

As the approaching sun reddened the eastern horizon, Rusty was snoring, but Patrick had now accepted that the information

Gideon had relayed to him about the fort's defences was correct.

He rolled to his feet and flexed his legs, freeing the cramps that his hours of sitting on watch had induced.

One careful pace at a time, Patrick edged from their position towards the fort. At the end of the tree-line he paused a moment, confirming that nobody was looking over the stockade, then dashed to the ditch. Again, he paused, then hurried to the stockade. With his back to the fence, he edged to the gap in the stockade and rolled over the broken logs.

A sharp pain ripped through his chest as he folded over the timbers, but he gritted his teeth and crawled past the powder magazine until he reached the parade ground entrance. He peered round the side of the stable.

In the parade ground, seven men were asleep before him. Gideon and Hannah lay to the side.

The powder magazine was at his side.

121

Although Gideon hadn't seen where Jack had hidden the gold, Patrick guessed that it would be close to Jack.

He rolled to his feet and edged back along the stable wall, then paced into the open towards the magazine, but each pace grated on his ribs. He slipped his hand to his chest and felt dampness. He winced, reckoning that his rolling over the broken stockade and crawling on his belly had caused the damage.

He took a shallow, grating breath and continued his steady progress. Five yards from the powder magazine, he unholstered his gun and held the cold metal pressed against his cheek.

Loud footfalls sounded, approaching from behind.

Patrick flinched and peered around. He saw a shadow-filled indentation in the stable wall. Seeing no other choices, Patrick scurried back ten paces and slipped into the darkness. There, he listened to the guard's footsteps clump towards him.

Patrick closed his eyes and slipped his gun

beneath his jacket to reduce the reflections he was providing in the dark. To his relief, the footsteps paced past his position and continued round the powder magazine.

For long moments he stood, breathing shallowly, but when the footfalls had receded to silence, he wheezed in a long gasp of air, which grated through his lungs.

He slipped from the indentation, but then swayed and fell back against the stable wall. Nausea blasted into his guts. He threw his head back and wheezed deep breaths, forcing down the urge to vomit. By degrees the nausea subsided, but it left his skin with a cold, clammy sheen.

He passed his gun to his other hand and flexed his fingers, freeing the cramps, then stood tall.

With his head held high, he stumbled to the powder magazine and stood beside the doorway. He listened for snoring or heavy breathing from within, but only heard the other men shifting in their sleep in the parade ground.

He moved to slip into the powder magazine, but another wave of dizziness knocked him back against the wall. He gripped his hand so tightly his fingernails bit into his palm, and moment by moment the nausea and the buzzing in his ears subsided. Then he swung round the doorway and inside.

In a series of frantic darting movements, he aimed his gun into each corner of the room, but aside from a turned-back blanket set before a saddle, the room was empty.

Another doorway led into a second room.

He stalked across the first room to this doorway and peered around the side. Stacked against the back wall was the pile of bags that until a few days ago had been his and Rusty's property.

This sight blasted all thoughts of caution from his mind and he strode into the room. When he reached the opposite wall, he slammed his hands on his hips and glared down at the bags.

'They're all there,' a voice said from the side.

Patrick swung to the side, arcing his gun towards the voice, but a gunshot ripped his gun from his hand, the sound deafening in the small room. He wrung his hand, then stood tall, peering into the darkness.

The voice had come from the shadows in the corner.

'Show yourself,' Patrick muttered. 'So that I...'

Sharp pain ripped into his chest again and Patrick staggered forward a pace, clutching his guts.

'So that you can see the man who kills you?'

'I...' Patrick fell to his knees.

He looked up. Jack emerged from the shadows, his gun appearing first as it caught a stray early-morning beam of light. His wide grin appeared next, then his solitary gleaming right eye.

In his left hand Jack clutched a card – the jack of diamonds.

'A one-eyed card said you'd get the gold. A non-face card said you'd get another bullet in the guts, but you got reasonably lucky.' Jack grinned and slipped the card into his top pocket. 'We get to fight it out.'

Jack hefted his gun, then hurled it into the shadows. As it clattered to a standstill, he raised his fists and advanced a long pace on Patrick.

With still staring at Jack, Patrick ensured he noted where the gun had landed. He couldn't see it, but it was roughly in the corner of the room.

He took a deep breath and staggered to his feet. With his feet planted wide, he stood as tall as he could.

'Come on,' he muttered. 'I've suffered enough. I'm ready to hand out punishment.'

Jack chuckled. 'You ain't suffered nearly as much as you will.'

With an arrogant flexing of a fist, Jack beckoned Patrick towards him.

Anger abated Patrick's pain and he raised his fists, then advanced three measured paces and hurled a left jab at Jack's chin.

Easily, Jack swayed back and with Patrick

off-balance, slammed a round-armed punch into Patrick's jaw.

Patrick's head snapped back, but he shrugged off the blow and stormed in, flailing his fists.

Again Jack swayed from the blows, but when Patrick moved in closer, he blasted a short-armed jab into Patrick's guts.

Patrick saw the blow coming and tried to roll with it. But it still ripped the air from his lungs.

Ruptured flesh and muscle tore as Patrick folded over the punch. Jack held his fist tight against Patrick's guts, his one eye bright.

Through pain-racked eyes, Patrick watched Jack grin and thrust his fist in even deeper. Then, with no control of his movements, he staggered back, doubled over. He fell to his knees, then keeled over on to his back.

For long moments he lay on his back, his guts sticky. Then, gathering all his strength, he rolled on to his front and slammed both hands to the ground. He tried to stand, but his weak arms couldn't lift his body an inch.

Jack wandered around him, grinning.

'You ain't got much fight in you.' He shrugged. 'Guess that's why you lost your showdown with Rusty Anderton.'

Jack advanced a long pace and kicked Patrick in the chest.

Patrick rolled with the kick and kept rolling, trying to head towards the direction Jack had thrown his gun, but a firm foot slammed down on his chest, halting him.

Jack looked down at him a moment, then lifted his other leg and walked over him, grinding his foot deep into his guts.

This time, Patrick only heard the crunch of bone and felt nothing more as merciful oblivion overcame him.

CHAPTER 12

Gideon watched the group of men gather round the powder-magazine doorway at the side of the parade ground. They peered inside and gibbered as they slapped each other on their backs.

A gunshot had awoken Gideon, but as he now reckoned that the noise didn't come from Salvador attacking at sun-up, he used the distraction and rolled closer to Hannah to quiz her about what she'd told Jack. He confirmed that aside from Hannah's relaying the tale that they were kin, Jack had shown no interest in why he was here.

Then Gideon shrugged his blanket to his chin and tried to ignore the noise. Then from out of the hubbub he heard Strang shout: 'Patrick'. He lowered the blanket and glanced at Hannah.

She shrugged. 'Surely not.'

Gideon winced. 'That bull-headed idiot is capable of anything.'

He jumped to his feet and dashed to the powder magazine. He couldn't see into the building, but he shoved the gathered men aside until he could slip into the doorway.

In the doorway to the second room, Jack stood over Patrick's body. He was grinning as he ripped back his foot ready to slam yet another kick into Patrick's prostrate form.

'What are you doing?' Gideon shouted.

Jack lowered his foot and glanced over his shoulder. He shrugged.

'This man tried to sneak in here and kill me.'

Gideon dragged himself free to stand before Jack.

'And what are you doing now?'

'Teaching him that he made a mistake.'

Gideon glanced down at Patrick. Blood coated his chest. His swollen face was slack.

Gideon winced and shook his head.

'I reckon you have done that. He looks

dead already.'

Jack grabbed Patrick's collar and dragged his limp body up.

'You dead yet?' he roared, but when Patrick's head lolled back in his grip, he turned back to Gideon, his one eye wide and wild. 'He says he's still alive and he ain't learnt his lesson yet.'

Jack bunched a fist and hurled back his arm.

'Don't do that,' Gideon muttered.

Jack glanced at Gideon's waist, as always lacking a gunbelt, then at the semicircle of men standing behind him beyond the doorway.

'How will *you* stop me?'

'Hannah said that you're a decent man. I wasn't sure if she was right, but I gave you the benefit of the doubt. But if she sees what you're doing, she'll lose her doubts, and even if she doesn't, I will.'

Jack glanced away a moment, breathing deeply. Then, with a snap of his wrist, he released Patrick for him to slump on his back.

He reached into his top pocket and extracted his pack of cards. As he hefted them in his right hand, he mouthed to himself, then nodded.

Several men behind Gideon started a low mutter.

'Cards, cards, cards.'

With his gaze set firmly on Gideon, Jack ripped a card from the pack and showed it to him.

Gideon glanced at the king of clubs.

'What does that mean?'

With a flick of the wrist, Jack turned the card over and chuckled.

'It says Patrick lives.' He moved to leave the powder magazine, then turned and jabbed a firm finger at Gideon. 'Once you've doctored him, tell him that if he annoys me again, I'll ask another card. And I've learnt one thing about random chance – a man can't beat the odds for ever.'

Jack brushed past Gideon. His men cleared a path for him, then followed him into the parade ground.

While the men cleared away, Gideon dashed across the room and knelt beside Patrick. He checked that he was still breathing, then rolled back on his haunches, shaking his head.

The faint light darkened and Gideon glanced to the side.

Hannah stood in the doorway watching Jack's receding back, then turned to face Gideon.

'Did you hear any of what happened in here?' Gideon asked.

'No,' she said, 'but...'

'But you can see that Patrick needs help.'

She glanced at Patrick's body and winced, then hitched her skirts and dashed into the powder magazine to kneel beside Patrick.

'What happened?' she asked.

Gideon glanced over his shoulder at the pile of bags lying in the second room.

'Patrick tried to reclaim the gold Jack stole from him, I guess.'

Gideon levered Patrick's jacket aside and appraised the blood-soaked bandages beneath. 'Then your fascinating man reversed the good work we'd done for Patrick.'

Hannah gulped. 'Jack had to defend himself.'

'Yeah, but he had no right to enjoy himself while he did that.' Gideon stared at Hannah, but as she met his gaze, he levered his hands under Patrick's shoulders. 'Come on. Help me get Patrick somewhere more comfortable.'

To avoid yet another irritating shake of the shoulder from Gideon, Patrick opened his eyes. He blinked away his blurred vision to see that Gideon was peering down at him. Hannah was at his side.

'This is getting to be a habit,' Patrick whispered.

Gideon nodded. 'And not one I enjoy.'

Gideon passed a bandage to Hannah, who held it up by the only corner that wasn't soaked in blood.

Patrick gulped. 'How bad?'

'How bad do you reckon it should be after

that escapade?'

'Just tell me,' Patrick snapped.

'You'll live. But you'll answer my question. What do you think you were doing?'

Patrick glanced away from Gideon's accusing glare to look around the bare room, then through the doorway into the parade ground beyond. From this angle, he guessed that he was in the officers' quarters beside the gate. And as the few men he could see sauntering around weren't looking his way, he guessed that nobody considered him dangerous.

He turned back to face Gideon.

'I was getting back my gold.'

'You were badly injured even before you burst in here. You could barely move around, never mind take on the men in here and Salvador's men.'

'I run from no man.'

'I know. And now you can barely walk.'

Patrick glared at Gideon, then produced a low chuckle.

'Perhaps you're right. I wasn't thinking too clearly.'

'That pretty much sums up your life. But perhaps it was worth it just so you could learn some sense.' Gideon prodded Patrick's bruised cheek. 'Where's Rusty?'

Patrick bunched his jaw as he suppressed a wince.

'Don't know and I don't care.'

With Hannah's help, Gideon levered Patrick up and wrapped a fresh blanket around his chest.

'You two must have sorted out your differences enough to work together, surely?'

'I never said that,' spat Patrick as Gideon lowered him to the ground. He bit his bottom lip as Gideon pulled the bandage tight. 'I tried to forgive him, but every time I looked at him I saw someone I can't trust any more.'

'He saved your life.' Gideon slipped a finger under a bandage to confirm it was tight enough. 'And you should trust someone who does that.'

'I might have done, eventually, but at gunpoint he told me the truth.' Patrick forced his lips into a grim smile. 'Rusty shot me accidentally while he was aiming at someone else.'

Gideon leaned back, his eyebrows raised.

'That isn't too bad. Can't blame a man for having poor aim.'

'I can't. And if Rusty had told me that straight away, I'd have forgiven him without thinking, but he hid that mistake with a stupid lie, and after he did that, I can never trust him again.'

Gideon nodded and glanced at Hannah.

'Fetch me some more water, please,' he said with a smile.

Hannah glanced at the bulging skin of water at her feet. She shrugged, then grabbed it and scurried to the door.

Patrick watched her leave, then turned back to Gideon.

'You still intent on rescuing the whore?'

'Her name is Hannah,' Gideon snapped, 'and she's helped to nurse you back to health – twice.'

'All right. I'm sorry. You still intent on

rescuing Hannah?'

'Yeah.'

'You're wasting your time. She ain't–'

Gideon pulled hard on Patrick's bandage, dragging a wince from him.

'I'm not questioning your desire to get your gold, and I'm not looking for advice on my motivations.'

Patrick nodded, but for long moments he contemplated Gideon.

'But do I really need water?'

'No.' Gideon provided a thin smile. 'But at the moment I don't know where her loyalties lie.'

Patrick edged up on to one elbow.

'Does that mean you have a plan?'

Gideon laid a hand on Patrick's shoulder and pushed him down.

'Not yet. But Jack is staying here, so we have time.'

'What about Salvador? From the sound of it, he has even less patience than I have.'

'I hope to delay him attacking until the right time.'

Patrick nodded. 'And when is the right time?'

Gideon rolled back on his haunches and blew out his cheeks.

'Two minutes after I've devised a plan to get me and Hannah out of here.' He patted Patrick's shoulder. 'Now I need to think, so lie back and pretend you're in plenty of pain and that you're too weak to do anything.'

Patrick rubbed his chest and winced.

'I reckon I can do that.'

'Why did you beat Patrick that badly?' Hannah muttered as she walked into the powder magazine.

Jack glanced up, his one eye now tired and cold.

'Because he tried to kill me.'

Hannah placed the skin of water at her feet.

'But you were vicious. That ain't your way.'

'You don't know me well enough to say that.'

'But I know you do nothing without careful consideration. And beating Patrick like that required real anger. Why did he annoy you that much?'

Jack rolled to his feet and stalked across the room to face Hannah.

'I hate people who double-cross me.' Jack extracted the pack of cards from his top pocket and fanned them out. 'So I took a card and it told me to beat him. Later, I took another card and it told me to stop beating him.'

'The cards. It always comes down to those damn cards.' Hannah slammed a fist against her thigh, but then closed her eyes a moment to abate her anger. 'You're the most resolute man I've ever met. Why do you let the cards rule your life?'

Jack extracted a card from the pack and glanced at it. He smiled.

'You can't control random chance. To win at the rest, you need to constantly check that you're still a winner.'

Jack extracted a second card, but when he moved to turn it over, Hannah thrust out a hand and held the card down, away from his gaze.

'But why do you decide on matters of love by asking the cards? Surely you must know what's in your own heart.'

Jack snorted and ripped his hand from Hannah's grip, but he still held the card face down.

'For matters of the heart, the cards are the only way.' Jack thrust the other cards into his top pocket and lowered his voice to a whisper as his one eye darted away from its intense appraisal of Hannah.

'Every woman I've ever cared for left me on the turn of a card.'

Hannah gulped. 'Have there been many others?'

Jack chuckled as he licked his lips and returned his gaze to Hannah.

'Two.'

'Including me?' Hannah forced a smile. She searched Jack's one eye, but it was blank. 'But it can't include me. You've already asked the cards and they said I'd stay.'

'Really?' Jack lifted the card, showing her the six of spades, then returned it to his pocket.

Hannah bit her bottom lip, then stood tall.

'What was the other woman's name?'

Jack swung round and stalked to the back wall. He thrust up both hands and laid them flat on the wall, then swung his weight down as he hung his head.

'Amber,' he whispered.

'Is she still—'

'Don't go there,' Jack snapped. He took long, deep breaths and when he spoke his voice was tired. 'Amber went to a man called Wilton Knox.'

With a hand lifted to place it on Jack's shoulder, Hannah edged two paces closer to Jack, then stopped and slipped her hand down to her side.

'And do you still care for—'

'Enough of this,' Jack snapped, slamming his fist against the wall. 'You know something about me. And I ain't sure if I'm happy that another woman knows my weakness.'

Hannah smiled and tiptoed to Jack's side. She extracted the pack of cards from his top pocket.

'Then I'll see what the cards say you'll do with me,' she whispered.

CHAPTER 13

With Patrick cared for and now resting, Gideon took a wander around the raised platform.

From under lowered brows, the guards, Strang and Don, watched him approach with apparent lack of concern. As he passed, they nodded to him and when he'd reached the corner of the platform Gideon chanced to glance back, but they weren't looking his way.

Even with their seeming trust that he wouldn't leave the fort, Gideon didn't dare try to sneak out during daylight hours. So he had to continue hoping that Salvador would be patient for the rest of the day.

Directly behind the powder magazine, he climbed down a ladder to ground-level. He crept past the pile of rotting timber that littered the corner of the fort, perhaps the remnants of a bastion, and faced the back of the powder magazine. From his casual consideration of the formidable building, he saw no way to get into it other than through the main door.

He turned and stalked to the timber pile. There, he sat, hunched his knees to his chin, and wondered yet again how he might escape with Hannah when the shooting started.

'Gideon,' someone whispered.

Gideon glanced around, but, on seeing no one, he shook his head and stood.

'Gideon.' The voice was more insistent now. Gideon peered around until his gaze fell on the timber pile. With his brow furrowed, he climbed on to a large log and gazed across the tangle of rotting timber.

Half-way to the stockade, a face was peering at him through a gap between two logs. A hand was beckoning him to approach.

He clambered over logs until, with his hands on his knees, he could peer into the shadow-filled hole. The man was Rusty.

'How did you get in?' Gideon asked, hunkering down beside the hole.

'Easy,' Rusty whispered. 'I was the miner in my partnership with Patrick. Show me a secure place and I'll find a way to get in.'

Gideon sighed and glanced around, but from his limited view of the parade ground, he couldn't see either of the guards.

'Assume you know about Patrick.'

Rusty hung his head for a moment.

'Tell me the worst.'

'He's alive, but when he tried to reclaim the gold, Jack caught him and beat him.' Gideon shook his head. 'He won't be trying any more damn fool missions like last night's for a while.'

'Where is he?'

'In the officers' quarters.' Gideon pointed to the parade ground where the edge of the building was just visible beside the gate.

'I'll get him out.'

'Don't risk that.'

'I ain't as bull-headed as Patrick is. I'll be careful.'

'But why? He has no interest in working with you.'

Rusty glared at the logs below him and rolled on to his side. He hurled a stone down the timber heap, then took a long breath and turned back to face Gideon.

'He's my friend.' Rusty lowered his head and rubbed the back of his neck. 'I have to try.'

Gideon leaned down to the hole and patted Rusty's shoulder.

'You're a good man. I wish Patrick had a tenth of the decency you have.'

'He ain't that bad.' Rusty frowned. 'So, will you help me?'

Gideon hung his head a moment, then glanced over his shoulder. Still, he could see nobody in the parade ground and the guards on the raised platform were out of his view. But the guards' steady patrol had to reach this spot before too much longer.

'Sure.' Gideon watched Rusty smile, but then raised a hand. 'But that help's on one condition – you help me get Hannah out.'

Rusty nodded and held out a hand from his hole.

'Deal.'

Gideon shook the hand. 'So how are we–'

'What you doing?' someone yelled from behind him.

As Rusty rolled into the shadows, Gideon swirled round to face Strang, who stood at the bottom of the timber pile and was glaring at him with his hands on his hips.

'You were being quiet to sneak to up on me,' Gideon said, smiling.

'You weren't. Who were you talking to?'

'Myself.' Gideon shrugged and sauntered three paces down the timber pile. 'Nobody else talks to me much so I have to talk to myself.'

Strang peered around, but Rusty had disappeared into his bolthole. Still, Strang stalked up the timber pile.

With his brow knotted, Strang ran his gaze over the logs, then settled on a hole, but not the one from which Rusty had emerged. He hunkered down to stare into it, but then shook his head and stood to face Gideon.

'And did that nobody head off down this hole?'

'You must have heard me rooting around. The hole doesn't go anywhere.' Gideon considered Strang's sneer. 'It's far too cramped in there, but if you don't believe me, try getting into it yourself.'

'Quiet.' Strang grabbed Gideon's arm and dragged him a pace towards the powder magazine. 'I reckon I'll let Jack ask you that question.'

CHAPTER 14

Strang dragged Gideon into the powder magazine and pushed him forward to face Jack. Hannah wasn't there.

'What was he doing?' Jack grunted as he looked up.

'He was talking to someone from outside the fort,' Strang muttered.

Jack winced. 'Who?'

'Don't know. Don and Brady are scouting around, but I reckon he's long gone. But Gideon was talking to someone.' Strang kicked Gideon forward a pace and grinned. 'And I reckon you might enjoy asking him who.'

'I would.' Jack turned his cold, one-eyed gaze on Gideon. 'Who were you talking to?'

Gideon hung his head for a moment. Any detailed examination of the collapsed building was sure to find the hole Rusty had used to get in. And from Gideon's experience of the inevitable logic of the likes of Jack Wolf, this discovery would only lead to one result.

'Salvador Milano,' he said, settling for a lie that wouldn't cause trouble for Patrick and Rusty.

Jack nodded. 'He was that uppity varmint in Destitution. Why is he here?'

Gideon rubbed his jaw.

'This will take some explaining.'

'Take your time.' Jack licked his lips, then fingered his gunbelt. 'You got the rest of your life.'

Gideon took a deep breath.

'Back in Destitution, Salvador overheard Hannah and me talking about the gold you'd just got. He waylaid me. He told me he'd kill us both unless I helped him get the gold from you.'

Jack's only eye twitched.

'You and Hannah are betraying me.'

'Not Hannah. She knows nothing of my deal with Salvador.'

Jack snorted, his hand drifting down to his holster.

'You know what happens to people who double-cross me?'

'I can guess, but I haven't double-crossed you.' Gideon glanced away from Jack a moment, then sighed. 'And I reckon you have feelings for Hannah and she won't return those feelings to you if you kill her brother.'

For long moments Jack glared at Gideon, then pointed a firm finger at Strang.

'Fetch Hannah,' he grunted.

As Strang scurried outside, Gideon sauntered to the side wall and leaned against it, trying to appear nonchalant and to hide the fact that his palms were sweating and his heart was pounding. But even when he'd leaned against the wall, Jack was still glaring at him.

'Don't be angry with her,' Gideon said. 'She knows nothing about any of this.'

'I ain't angry with *her.*'

A minute later, Strang paced back into the powder magazine with Hannah in tow. She

151

glanced at Jack, then at Gideon.

'What's happened?' she asked.

Jack flashed Gideon a harsh glare, then folded his arms.

'Your brother was talking to someone who'd sneaked into the fort.'

A strangulated cry escaped Hannah's lips before she threw her hand to her mouth, but through her fingers a screeched word still emerged.

'Who?'

Gideon pushed from the wall. 'She knows–'

'Quiet!' Jack roared. 'You ain't prompting her. I want Hannah to tell me what she knows.'

Hannah kneaded her brow, then held her hands wide and stared at the ground before Jack's feet.

'I have no idea,' she whispered, 'about anything that Gideon has done to double-cross you. But he doesn't know anyone around here but me.'

'Not even Salvador Milano?'

Hannah's mouth fell open. She winced and flashed a glare at Gideon, then turned back to Jack.

'I don't...' A single tear escaped her right eye and rolled down her cheek. She brushed it away, then snuffled.

'You don't cry,' Jack muttered. 'But as you are, I can see that you didn't know what a double-crossing piece of scum your brother is.'

Gideon took a deep breath and pushed from the wall.

'I'm sorry, Hannah,' he said. 'Salvador made me help him.' Gideon placed his hands together and held them out to Jack. 'If you want to blame someone, blame me.'

'I do,' Jack grunted.

With his gaze set on Gideon, Jack ripped a random card from his top pocket and held it high, then swirled it round.

The card was the ten of hearts.

Gideon gulped.

'Does that card say I live or die?'

Jack thrust the card into his pocket. His

hand strayed towards his holster, then lifted to rub his chin.

'It says you get a chance to live.'

Using the route he'd found the previous night, Gideon sneaked from the fort, this time under the watchful gaze of Strang and Don. Once in the forest, he leaned against a tree and took long deep breaths, calming his nerves after his lucky escape.

Then he edged through the trees until he reached Salvador's camp. He relayed the news that Strang had found a stash of whiskey in the fort and that Jack's men were planning to drink a good quantity of it that afternoon.

Without question, Salvador accepted this news and he readily decided on the choice, popular with his followers, of attacking at sundown.

Gideon then hurried back to the fort. He relayed news of the success of his mission to Strang, who grunted his displeasure at Gideon's continued survival, then moseyed into the powder magazine to see Jack.

Left on his own, Gideon glanced around the parade ground. Hannah was sitting huddled under her blanket by the stable wall. Gideon wavered for a moment, then joined her.

For long moments he stood before her, but when she continued to stare at the ground, pointedly ignoring his presence, he sat beside her. Still, she didn't look at him.

'I'm sorry,' he whispered.

'Me too,' she murmured. She turned her cold gaze on Gideon. 'You followed me here to save me, but you're determined to get me killed.'

'Like I said, I'm sorry. I was just trying to help.'

Hannah shook her head, but her stern expression softened and she shuffled a foot closer to Gideon.

'Accepted.' She lowered her voice. 'But just let me do the talking from now on and we'll both survive Salvador's ambush.'

Gideon nodded, but he took a deep breath.

'I have to ask this – are you planning to survive the ambush with Jack or without him?'

Hannah glanced away, biting her lip.

'I don't know.'

Gideon drew his legs to his chest.

'You could do better than him.'

'In my life, I don't meet men that are any better than Jack.'

'Then change your life.'

'You mean be a doctor?'

'It's a caring profession. And you care about people.'

'I don't reckon I care as much as you do.'

Gideon sighed and laid a hand on her arm for a moment.

'Then do whatever you want to do, but hanging on to a man like Jack isn't the answer.'

Hannah rubbed at her arm as she breathed deeply through her nostrils. Then she flared her eyes and opened her mouth to utter a sharp retort, but Strang was now sauntering across the parade ground and

Gideon raised a hand, silencing her.

Strang pointed to the powder magazine and grinned at Hannah.

'Jack wants you,' he grunted, then leered at her as he licked his lips.

Hannah stood. She looked down at Gideon as she smoothed her skirt.

'I'll determine that myself, Gideon.' Hannah turned and walked away after Strang, her skirts swinging.

'Be careful,' Gideon said, but Hannah kept her gaze set forward and strode across the parade ground.

In the doorway to the powder magazine Hannah waited until Strang wandered off, then paced inside.

Jack was in the second room, sitting against the wall in a rectangle of light, the bags of gold at his back, the pack of cards held loosely in his right hand.

'What do you want?' she asked.

'I want an answer.' He looked up, his one eye cold. 'Who is Gideon?'

'My brother.'

'He doesn't look like you, and neither does he look at you like a sister.'

Hannah gulped. 'He hasn't seen me for a while, perhaps he ain't used to seeing me all grown up.'

Jack tossed the pack of cards to his left hand.

'Perhaps.'

Hannah cocked her head to one side and lowered her voice to its softest tone.

'Did Amber burn the trust from your heart? Did Amber hurt you so badly that you don't want to touch me? Did Amber stop you making decisions? Did Amber force you to ask the cards about everything?'

Jack patted a firm finger on the top of the cards.

'I decide my own fate.'

'The cards decide your fate.' Hannah edged another pace closer to Jack. 'Did Wilton Knox force you to avoid making decisions?'

'It wasn't him.' Jack hung his head for a moment. For some time he contemplated the cards in his hand, then looked up, his one eye glazed and possibly no longer seeing this room.

'It was me.'

Hannah knelt beside Jack. She lifted his right hand and cradled it in both her hands.

'Just tell me. You can trust me.' She smiled. 'The cards say you can.'

Jack looked at her, a line of moisture brimming his eye.

'I got into a poker-game with Wilton Knox in Black Rock. On one hand, the stakes got higher and higher. Neither of us would back down. I bet every last cent I had, plus a few that I didn't, but Wilton matched me. To call him, I had to risk the most precious thing in the world.' Jack slipped his hand from Hannah's grasp. 'My woman.'

'You bet a person on a hand of poker?' Hannah stared at Jack, seeing him nod. 'And you lost?'

'Sure did. But that ain't the worst of it. She went through with the deal.'

'I don't understand.'

159

'Amber and me were a team. We planned to steal the money I lost that night. She was going to lead Wilton on, then when his guard was down, kill him. But she didn't. She stayed. She said she could only love a winner.' Jack rubbed his ruined orbit. 'So I killed her.'

For long moments Hannah sat in silence. Then she rolled to her feet and edged across the room to look through the door into the other room.

'I'm sorry for you,' she whispered. She turned back and folded her arms. 'But I don't see why you still ask the cards.'

Jack held up the pack of cards and fanned them out.

'I have to prove that I'm still a winner, because the moment the cards turn against me again, I'll lose everything.'

Hannah stalked across the room and pushed his hand down. She closed her small hand over his, crushing the cards into a solid deck.

'Trust people, not the cards.' She held her

other hand to her heart. 'Trust me, not the cards.'

'I can't.' Jack's one eye darted up to appraise her. 'I keep wondering why you're here.'

'You know why.'

'I don't. Are you here for the gold? Is Gideon here for the gold? Is Gideon working with Salvador to get the gold?'

'That's a lot of questions. Why not ask the cards?' She snorted and lifted her hand. 'You trust them more than you trust me.'

'Perhaps I will.' Jack fanned out his cards and extracted one. He moved to turn it over, but Hannah grabbed his hand.

'But after this one time, don't ask them again.'

Jack nodded and turned the card over. He flashed a smile.

'The two of diamonds.'

'And what did you ask them?'

'I asked whether I should trust you.'

'And the answer?'

For long moments Jack stared at Hannah,

then shrugged.

'Leave me now,' he whispered. 'I'm sure your brother needs help tending Patrick's wounds.'

CHAPTER 15

'How do you feel?' Gideon asked.

Patrick opened his eyes to look at Gideon.

'Not good.' He coughed to clear his throat. 'What was that noise about earlier?'

Gideon hunkered down beside Patrick. He laid a hand on his brow, nodded, and removed the hand.

'It was Rusty.'

Patrick sneered. 'What's that no-good varmint doing now?'

'He tried to sneak into the fort and Strang saw him.'

Patrick raised his eyebrows, the hint of a smile on his lips.

'Did Jack kill him?'

'No. Rusty got away. But Jack nearly killed me.'

Patrick snorted and shook his head.

'I'm sorry. No other good men should suffer because of that man.'

'I talked with him. He's sorry. He wants you to trust him again.'

With a lunge, Patrick grabbed Gideon's collar and tried to lever himself to a sitting position, but when his guts twinged, he relented and lay back.

'I ain't ever trusting him again,' he grunted, his voice shallow. 'He lied to me.'

Gideon sighed and glanced away from Patrick, then rolled round to sit on the ground.

'He's determined to save your life, even if you've embarked on a determined effort to end it.'

Patrick rubbed his chest.

'You ain't making me feel any better about Rusty. That man's a repeated liar and a yellow-belly.'

Gideon opened his mouth to argue some more, but then decided that prolonging this discussion was just wasting his time and closed his mouth. With a long shake of his head, he stood.

'Then I'll just tell you this. Salvador Milano attacks at sundown.' Gideon glanced through the doorway. 'And that comes any minute now. Rusty will try to get you out. When—'

'I don't want him to save me,' Patrick snapped.

'Then you can discuss that with him, but in the confusion, you can either go for the gold, kill Rusty, or save yourself, but frankly, I don't care.' Gideon glanced down at the bandages encasing Patrick's chest. 'Whatever I do or say, you'll find some way to kill yourself.'

Gideon turned from Patrick and strode to the door.

'Thanks, Gideon,' Patrick shouted after him. 'My quarrel ain't with you. You're a good man.'

Gideon stopped. He rocked on his heels, then turned back and nodded.

'Obliged.'

Patrick took a deep breath. 'And I hope you can get that ... Hannah out safely.'

'Hope is all I have,' Gideon said, then departed from the room.

In the parade ground Jack's men had spread out, taking positions in the doorway to the powder magazine, hiding beside the stable, and at regular intervals along the raised platform. They'd left the gate unguarded.

Gideon joined Hannah and leaned against the stable wall facing the gate. Over the raised platform opposite, the sun had already edged below his view. Only the apex of the powder magazine's tin roof was catching the last red rays of the dying sun.

'Rider approaching,' Strang shouted from the raised platform.

'Everyone into position,' Jack shouted. He stalked along the side of the wall to Hannah's side. 'And you can stay with me in the powder magazine until the shooting's over.'

Hannah glanced at Gideon, then headed past Jack towards the powder magazine.

Gideon moved to follow her, but Jack grabbed his arm and shook his head.

'I can't help out here,' Gideon said.

'I reckon your doctoring skills might be useful any minute now.' Jack chuckled. 'If you live long enough.'

Gideon shrugged and hunkered down beside the stable wall, making his profile as small as possible.

From the ground he watched Strang crawl fast along the raised platform, then skid down the ladder with his feet on either side. He scurried across the parade ground towards the gate.

'It ain't Salvador,' Strang shouted over his shoulder. 'It's Leland.'

A subdued whoop emerged from around the parade ground as Strang swung the gate open to let Leland Ashley ride into the fort.

Strang immediately swung the gate closed, then tipped his hat to Leland.

'Mighty glad to see you're back,' he shouted. 'We reckoned you'd taken off.'

'Nope.' Leland swung down from his horse. 'I just had me some trouble.'

Leland dashed across the parade ground. Jack wavered a moment, then gestured for Hannah to head into the magazine alone.

'So where were you?' Jack asked, a huge grin emerging as he patted Leland's back.

'Tracked down Fernando and Cliff, but those gold-diggers got to them first. We had a mighty battle. They killed Tort and I only just got out of there alive.'

Jack kicked at the ground. 'I should never have let them live.'

'And I got some more bad news for you. Salvador Milano and a whole mess of troublemakers have followed you. I reckon he's planning to attack.'

'I know that.' Jack pointed at the men along the raised platform. 'We're just waiting for him.'

'How do you know about him?'

Jack strode to the stable wall, grabbed

167

Gideon's arm, and dragged him to his feet. He swung him round and pushed him forward.

'Gideon's helping us.'

'Him!' Leland looked Gideon up and down, shaking his head and sneering. 'He ain't reliable. Gideon is one of Salvador's followers. I saw him in the group when Tort and me passed them yesterday. He was riding alongside that whore you liked.'

Jack's one eye blazed. His jaw muscles tightened so hard they seemed set to burst.

'Get Hannah!' he roared, his voice echoing across the parade ground.

Strang chuckled, then scurried to the powder magazine.

'I can explain,' Gideon said, turning to Jack. 'I told you—'

'Be quiet!'

Jack swirled round and hurled a round-armed fist at Gideon. The blow slammed into his cheek and sent him sprawling.

On the ground Gideon moved to rise, then decided that that would only lead to another blow and lay back.

With a wide grin on his face, Strang dragged Hannah from the powder magazine and led her across the parade ground to Jack's side. He pushed her forward a pace, then with a last grin down at Gideon, scurried to the raised platform.

'Yeah,' Leland said with a snort, 'that's her. She was with Salvador too.'

Jack slammed his fist against his thigh and stalked around Hannah, looking her up and down.

Hannah stood tall and glanced at Gideon on the ground, but Gideon couldn't meet her gaze and looked away. The topmost part of the powder magazine had the faintest red glow of the sun and as he looked, it closed to nothing.

Jack swung to a standstill. His firm gaze washed over Hannah and rested on her eyes.

'You said you didn't know Salvador Milano,' he muttered, 'but Leland saw you riding with him. So no more lies, Hannah, are you working with Salvador?'

Hannah gulped. 'We did ride with Salvador. But everything else Gideon told you is the truth. We had no choice but to go with him.'

Jack nodded and glanced down at Gideon.

'And what's your story, Hannah's *brother*?'

Gideon took a deep breath and rolled to a sitting position.

'The same as my sister's. Salvador gave us no choice but to help him get the gold from you. But I don't care about helping him, and Hannah just wanted–'

'You don't tell me what Hannah wants.' Jack slammed a firm hand on Hannah's shoulder. 'She tells me. So, Hannah, look me in the eye and tell me the truth. Did you come here for the gold or for me?'

Hannah sighed and held her hands wide. The calmest and most benign of smiles spread across her face.

'There's only one thing I want, and you must know what–'

'Salvador,' Jack muttered, staring over

Hannah's shoulder.

Hannah glared at Jack a moment. Then she and everyone else turned to the raised platform.

Strang was gesturing down at them with a circular motion above his head – the signal that Salvador's assault was starting.

'Positions everyone,' Jack muttered.

CHAPTER 16

On his back, Patrick Grady listened to the men outside the officers' quarters scurry around the parade ground. From the sudden drop in the light streaming in from outside, he guessed that Salvador's assault was imminent.

He prodded his chest, but the flesh was no sorer than before, so he rolled to his knees.

A clatter sounded in the adjoining room, as of someone jumping to the ground. Then footsteps paced towards him. He looked to the side. Rusty stood in the doorway to the second room.

'You,' Patrick spat. 'Get away from me.'

Rusty stalked to Patrick's side and slammed a hand over his mouth.

'Be quiet or you'll get us both killed.'

Patrick glared at Rusty, then shrugged out from beneath the hand.

'How did you get in here?' he whispered.

'I'm a miner. I'll sneak through any hole to get where I want to go. I have a way into the fort, and that means I have a way out.'

'Gideon said. But I don't care. I ain't leaving without the gold.'

Rusty rolled back and appraised Patrick from head to foot.

'You ain't in a state to fight anyone.'

'I'll take on...' Patrick narrowed his eyes as Rusty extracted a pad from his pocket and slammed it over his mouth.

Patrick threw his hands to Rusty's hand and tried to prise the fingers from his mouth, but Rusty pressed down even harder. Thick,

172

cloying fumes invaded his nostrils and ripped through his senses.

As his fingers numbed, his vision blurred, then darkened.

On the raised platform Strang was gesturing feverishly.

Gideon didn't know what the gestures meant, but he guessed that Salvador was now on the other side of the gate.

As Jack's men scurried into hiding down in the parade ground, Jack glared at Hannah and Gideon in turn, then shook his head.

'I ain't got time to deal with you right now.' He glanced at Leland, then stalked towards the powder magazine. 'Tie them up.'

Leland grabbed Gideon's arm and dragged him to his feet.

Gideon slackened his arms and let Leland bundle him to the stable wall. There, Leland pulled his hands behind his back and wrapped a rope around his hands.

Hannah stood by Gideon's side and

placed her hands together before her, but when Leland had pulled Gideon's bonds tight, he batted her hands away, then dragged them behind her back.

When he'd tied Hannah too, he pushed them both to the ground and hurled a blanket over each of them, then dashed away to join Jack in the powder magazine.

'Gideon,' Hannah whispered, lying back and staring at the sky, 'you're an idiot. Your tales have destroyed the trust I'd built with Jack.'

'I'm sorry.'

'It's too late for that.' From the corner of her eye, she glared at Gideon, her gaze accusing. 'You came here to help me, but you've just ensured I don't get out of this alive.'

Gideon set his jaw firm, forcing this truth from his mind.

'Even if I wasn't here, Leland would still have seen you with Salvador and I reckon Jack would still have been unimpressed.'

Hannah sighed, but then provided a reluctant nod.

'Perhaps. But Jack doesn't believe you're my brother and–'

'Quit accusing me and start thinking how we can escape from this.'

Hannah turned to glance at the gate, then at the powder magazine.

'If you keep your mouth shut and let me talk, we might have a chance.'

'Suppose I deserve that.' Gideon glanced at the gate, from behind which he heard scuffling sounds, as of Salvador and his followers preparing to barge in. 'But if you're still talking to me, have you discovered anything about Jack that we can use?'

For long moments Hannah didn't reply. Then she sighed.

'Just one thing. And when I discovered it, I learned everything about him. But I'm not sure how it might help you.'

'We don't have much time. Don't keep it quiet.'

'It's not something I can tell you. It's something I can give you.'

Under her blanket, Hannah shuffled to

175

Gideon's side and clawed her hand into the waistband of her skirt, then rolled on to her side. She lay against Gideon and slipped something into his pocket.

'What was that?' he asked.

Hannah rolled back to lie separately. 'If they remove your bonds before Jack kills you, try to use it, otherwise it's no use.'

Gideon nodded. He glanced around the deserted parade ground. Fifty yards away, the fort gate swung open.

Gideon sighed and returned to staring at the sky.

Uneasy scraps of dreams invaded Patrick's mind. Then, a timeless period later, he opened his eyes. His vision was blurred, but he saw a face peering down at him. He blinked repeatedly until his vision focused.

Rusty stood over him, a pensive smile on his face.

'What did you do?' Patrick murmured.

'I saved your life – again.'

Patrick glanced around. He was no longer

in the fort. Trees surrounded him in a small clearing. Tethered beside him was his horse.

He sat and stretched. 'Where are we?'

'Far enough from the fort to be in no danger from Salvador's and Jack's fight. You can leave when that's over.'

'How can I trust anything you say?'

Rusty gulped and rubbed fingers through his thick beard.

'The truth is hard to tell. And it's hard to admit to yourself. Now that I've done that, my duty is clear.'

'What have you admitted?'

'That I'm a yellow-belly.'

Although Patrick heard the words that he'd waited days to hear, they still left a hollow feeling in his gut. He shrugged.

'What you did was weak,' he said, surprising himself with the gentleness of his tone. 'It doesn't make you a yellow-belly.'

'I'm a yellow-belly because I couldn't tell you the truth.' Rusty snorted. 'And even myself. But now, I reckon I can.' Rusty laid a hand on Patrick's shoulder. 'I did shoot you, but I shot you to save my own life.'

'You what?' Patrick roared, hurling Rusty's hand away.

'I didn't shoot you accidentally. You only lived because my hand was shaking. Jack let me live because he could see what I'd done in my eyes.'

As he glared at Rusty, Patrick clenched his fists so tightly the bones cracked.

'You're wrong if you reckon saving my life puts that right.'

Rusty hefted a bag from his pocket and dropped it at Patrick's feet.

'I know, but I got some of the gold here. And as for the rest...' Rusty tipped his hat, then turned and raised a hand. 'Now that I've freed my conscience, don't follow me. You ain't strong enough. Just take this gold and enjoy the rest of your life.'

Patrick rolled to his knees and with his vision still clouded with anger, he watched Rusty disappear into the trees. He took long deep breaths, then glanced at the horse, then at the bag of gold-dust at his feet. With a hand clutching his guts, he staggered to his feet and shuffled ten paces to his right.

From his new position he saw that Rusty was heading back to the fort.

Patrick glanced at his horse again. Then, with a shrug, he tottered after Rusty.

CHAPTER 17

One steady pace at a time, Mack and Rodrigo stalked into the fort. They took flanking positions, kneeling on either side of the gate, and roved their rifles back and forth.

Mack beckoned Salvador to follow them in and with their heads down, Salvador and the remainder of his followers slipped inside and scurried along the side of the stockade. To short hand gestures from Salvador, they took positions at ten-yard intervals, then hunkered down and aimed at the huddle of blankets where Gideon and Hannah lay.

But then Salvador waved his arms above his head and, with Mack and Rodrigo on either side of him, he dashed across the parade ground, keeping low.

Two yards in front of Gideon he skidded to a halt.

'Where are they?' he muttered.

'Sleeping off that batch of whiskey,' Gideon said.

Salvador nodded and glared at Hannah.

'And why ain't you keepin' Jack all happy and distracted?'

Hannah shrugged beneath her blanket. 'When you start firing I don't want to be anywhere near Jack.'

Salvador chuckled. 'You're a right sensible whore. Now, where's Jack?'

'Over there.' Hannah stretched her head to the side and pointed to the powder magazine with her chin.

'That so?' Salvador said, looking at Gideon.

'Yeah.' Gideon nodded towards the powder magazine. 'He's over there.'

Salvador turned towards the magazine, but then turned back and looked at Hannah, then Gideon, lying on their backs under their blankets. His eyes narrowed. He stalked to Gideon's side and kicked the blanket from him, then reached down and pulled him to his feet.

While muttering an angry oath, he swung him round to see the coils binding his hands.

'What in tarnation are you—'

A gunshot blasted Salvador's hat from his head forcing him to hurl himself to the ground and lie flat.

Gideon tottered, then let himself fall to the side.

With no cover available, Salvador glanced back and forth, then on his belly squirmed to the stable wall and pressed himself flat. Another shot ripped out and Mack clutched his chest, his fingers clawing at the redness seeping through his fingers.

Even before Mack had keeled over, gunfire was roaring from all directions as Jack's men blasted at Salvador's men from the advantage of their covered positions.

Within ten seconds, two more of Salvador's men collapsed. With no choice other than to find somewhere to make a stand, they split. Some dashed for the officers' quarters, Zane getting in shots that blasted the men on the raised platform to the ground, but the others made a desperate charge towards the powder magazine. Another man collapsed before the rest scurried inside. Then fierce gunfire ripped out in the powder magazine.

Through the magazine doorway, Gideon watched Salvador's men fighting hand to hand with Jack's men, and from the occasional body he saw fall to the ground, he judged that the attackers accounted for some of Jack's men. But after less than a minute, quiet descended on the powder magazine. Then Jack and Leland edged to the doorway and peered outside.

Outside the officer's quarters the remnants of Salvador's men wavered a moment, then scurried inside, a last volley of gunfire from Jack and Leland hurrying them on their way.

Gideon gritted his teeth, listening for the gunshot that would herald their discovery of Patrick in the building, but he didn't hear a shot.

A hand slammed on his shoulder.

He looked up to see Salvador looming over him. Then he slid down to lie beside him.

'You double-crossed me,' Salvador muttered in Gideon's ear.

'I'm tied up and helpless. That ain't the position of someone who's gaining from this.'

Salvador snorted and levered an arm around Gideon's chest, then pulled him to his feet. He gestured to Rodrigo, who scurried from the stable wall and skidded to a halt behind Hannah. He also levered her to her feet and with her held before him, he faced the powder magazine.

To Salvador's instructions, they edged into the parade ground.

'You'd better hope Jack still likes you and

the whore,' Salvador muttered, 'or I'll be draggin' your lifeless body for a long way.'

'Jack hates me.'

'Then start prayin' his aim's poor.'

Walking sideways, they stalked to the centre of the parade ground and, aside from the occasional high blast of gunfire from the officers' quarters, everyone stilled their fire.

'Jack Wolf,' Salvador roared when he was ten yards from the officers' quarters. 'I got your woman.'

'You ain't leaving here alive,' Jack shouted from the powder magazine.

Salvador backed one steady pace at a time until he stood in the doorway.

'You know what kind of deal I want. You got three minutes to tell me what I want to hear.'

Salvador nodded to Rodrigo and they backed into the building.

Inside, the darkness had grown. Gideon glanced around, noting that Patrick's blankets were scattered.

He counted through the men he'd seen fall

since Salvador had ambushed the fort, and he judged that there ought to be two or maybe three men in the building. But the room was bare.

Rodrigo and Salvador glanced around too.

'Check the other room,' Salvador muttered.

Rodrigo hurled Hannah to the ground, then stalked across the room and stood beside the doorway.

'Anybody in there?' he shouted.

The only sound was Salvador's muttering under his breath.

Rodrigo glanced back at Salvador. Then he flinched and at that moment, Gideon saw a blurred shape slam into Salvador – a man falling from the rafters above. The man landed heavily on Salvador's shoulders slamming him to the ground.

Gideon just had time to realize the man was Rusty, but by then Rusty and Rodrigo were both blasting at each other. Rusty fell to one knee, lead ripping into the wall behind him, then blasted again at Rodrigo. His shot was wild.

From the corner of his eye, Gideon saw Salvador scramble to his feet and arc his gun towards Rusty. In desperation, Gideon rolled to his feet and hurled himself at Salvador.

He slammed into Salvador's side and pushed him to the ground. Another shot from Rodrigo blasted over his head as they both fell, but a second shot slammed into Rusty's shoulder and spun him round.

Rusty's head crashed into the wall and with the blow he slid, boneless, to the ground.

Salvador squirmed out from beneath Gideon, then dragged him up on to his knees. Gideon struggled but with his hands tied behind his back, he could only jut his chin defiantly.

Salvador rolled his shoulders, then slammed a long punch to Gideon's jaw. As Gideon crashed on to his back, Salvador darted a glance at Rusty, but he was lying slack and slumped against the wall. Salvador sneered, grabbed Gideon's shoulder, and pulled him to his feet. He held him straight, then pummelled his cheek.

Gideon landed heavily, but his respite was short-lived as Salvador pulled him to his feet again only to slam a blow deep into his guts, then crash another blow to his jaw that sent him sprawling.

'Stop,' Hannah shouted.

Salvador snorted. 'Be quiet. When I break Gideon in two, I'll start on you.'

'You want to bargain with us,' she shouted. 'You won't get anything if you kill us.'

'My choice.' Salvador dragged Gideon to his feet and pushed him to Rodrigo. He spat on his fist and rolled his shoulders. 'Now, hold him up while I give my fists some exercise.'

Rodrigo chuckled. Then his mouth fell open in silent shock. He bundled Gideon away, but a gunshot blasted into his shoulder, spinning him round, and a second shot to the back knocked him flat.

Salvador swung round towards Rusty, who was grinning up at him. A single shot ripped into Salvador's chest.

Salvador's feet left the ground before he slammed down on his back, spread-eagled. He hurled his hands to the ground and levered himself up a foot, but another bullet ripped into his forehead.

Salvador twitched once, then lay flat.

From the ground, Gideon nodded to Rusty.

'Thought he'd killed you,' Gideon said.

Rusty rolled to his feet, clutching his shoulder. He winced, then shrugged.

'I just reckoned that playing dead had to get them closer to me. And as Patrick knows, I don't miss from five yards.'

Rusty dashed to Gideon's side. He tugged on his ropes, and with Gideon's squirming help, untied him.

As Rusty untied Hannah, Gideon edged to the doorway and glanced outside.

The parade ground was still deserted but after the gunfire in here, he guessed they had only another minute or two before Jack sent someone to see what was happening.

He turned back to face Rusty.

'Did you get Patrick out?' he asked.

'Yup,' Rusty said.

Gideon nodded, then turned to Hannah.

'I've been risking my life to save you, but you were right. I never consulted you on whether you wanted saving. So I reckon that now is the time to ask you. Do you want to leave with me and Rusty, or do you want to stay and take your chances with Jack?'

Hannah hung her head a moment, then looked up and appraised Gideon with a firm gaze.

'Maybe now is the time to head back to Destitution.'

Gideon nodded, then turned to Rusty.

'I assume you have a way out of here?'

'Several ways, actually.' Rusty batted his hands free of dust. 'But as you ain't miners, we'll have to take the long way.'

Rusty led them into the second room. There, he paced over the three scattered bodies and pointed to a trapdoor in the roof that led to the raised platform.

Gideon noted Rusty's bloodied shoulder, then stood before him and swung Hannah up on to his shoulders to push the trapdoor open. When she'd rolled on to the roof, Gideon jumped and grabbed the side of the door. With Hannah tugging on his shirt back he rolled over on to the roof. Then he thrust an arm down and helped Rusty, one-handed, on to the roof.

They lay a moment, orientating themselves.

The roof opened on to the raised platform. A three-foot-high fence ran the length of the platform, providing cover from the parade ground. To Rusty's instructions they crawled behind it with Rusty leading and Gideon at the back.

Periodically, the gaps between the logs were wider than normal and Gideon guessed that if anyone from below was looking their way, they couldn't help but see them, but he didn't linger to encourage that chance.

But at the corner of the fort, Gideon paused a moment to peer through a gap into the parade ground. Don was stalking around the far stockade, arcing in towards the officers' quarters. Leland was matching his stealth on the other side.

Gideon judged that they had less than a minute before they discovered their escape.

He hurried on to catch Hannah and Rusty.

When the raised platform passed behind the stable, they reached a ladder. They hurried down it and scurried through the stables to emerge facing the powder magazine. They grouped and on the count of three scurried across open ground to the side of the magazine, then dashed around the back until they reached the collapsed bastion where Gideon had seen Rusty earlier.

With Rusty leading, they clambered over the timber pile towards Rusty's bolt-hole.

Rusty dropped to his knees and waited a moment for Hannah and Gideon to join him, then edged into the hole. He'd crawled in for three feet, and had disappeared down to his knees, when he screeched, then backed out.

With a gun aimed at Rusty's head, Strang followed Rusty from the hole and stood to his full height.

'You,' he muttered, 'are going nowhere.'

CHAPTER 18

Strang pulled Rusty round so that his back was to him, slipped his gun from its holster, then pushed him forward a pace.

Rusty and Gideon shared a pained glance. Then with Strang two paces back and urging them on, Hannah, Rusty and Gideon strode around the magazine and into the parade ground.

There, the remainder of Jack's men were scurrying around, checking on each of Salvador's men. Aside from Jack, Gideon counted five men who were still alive.

Don had dragged Salvador's body into the open and Jack was standing over him, but to Strang's holler, Jack swaggered across the parade ground to face Hannah. Any hint of his former tolerance of her antics had gone as he glared at her with his one harsh eye.

'Trying to escape, eh, Hannah?' he muttered.

Hannah shrugged. 'I just wanted to get away from the shooting.'

Jack sneered his disbelief, then reached into his top pocket and extracted the pack.

'Don't,' Hannah said. 'You said you wouldn't ask the cards again whether you should trust me.'

'I did ask the cards if I should trust you.' Jack lowered his voice to a grating whisper. 'Trouble is, the cards said I shouldn't.'

Hannah gulped with a pronounced sound. 'You got me wrong, Jack.'

Jack snorted and glanced at Rusty.

'Suppose that was your work in the officers' quarters?'

'Yeah,' Rusty said, jutting his chin. 'I killed

Salvador for you.'

Jack nodded. 'Obliged. The only question is – am I grateful enough to let you three live?'

Rusty shrugged. 'Suppose you'll ask the cards.'

'Yeah.' Jack glanced around his diminished troop of men, grinning.

'Cards, cards, cards,' Leland said, clapping his hands and looking around, smiling. Eventually his good cheer forced the others to join him.

'Cards, cards, cards,' Jack's men intoned. 'Cards, cards, *cards*.'

Jack held the pack aloft.

'A non-face card says you all die. A two-eyed card says only Hannah lives.' Jack licked his lips. 'A one-eyed card says you all live.'

Gideon sighed. 'Those ain't good odds.'

'Yeah,' Hannah muttered. 'You can't give us those odds.'

For long moments Jack glared at Hannah, then fanned the cards and held them out to her.

'But I have,' he said. 'Take a card. It's your only option.'

With her gaze set firmly on Jack, Hannah edged a pace towards him.

'Wait!' a voice shouted.

Everyone glanced to the side to see Patrick stagger out from beside the powder magazine. Blood soaked his jacket and he was stumbling with every pace, but he'd aimed his gun squarely at Jack's head.

'You again,' Jack muttered.

'Yeah,' Patrick said. 'Now move away.'

Jack folded his arms and faced off to Patrick.

'You're facing six men. You ain't in a position to order us.'

'I ain't giving orders. I just want to kill Rusty.' Patrick flinched. Pain creased his face, but as Leland feinted for his gun, Patrick wrestled the gun back into his hand and turned it on Leland. 'And nobody takes me before Rusty dies.'

Leland glanced at Jack, and to Jack's nod, he strode to Rusty's side. He grabbed

Rusty's arms and swung him round to face Patrick.

Without complaint, Rusty let Leland manhandle him and faced Patrick with his chin held high.

'You can't kill Rusty in cold blood, Patrick,' Gideon shouted.

Patrick staggered forward a pace. He raised his gun and aimed it firmly at Rusty's head.

'And I reckon I can.'

'Wait!' Gideon shouted. 'I know you, Patrick. You're a bull-headed idiot who doesn't think things through, but you're a decent man.'

From the corner of his eye, Patrick glanced at him.

'I can't let Rusty live.'

'And he probably won't. If the cards say Rusty should die, let that be on Jack's conscience, not yours.'

'Killing Rusty won't tear me up for long.' Patrick glanced around the semicircle of men facing him. 'From the look of things, none of us will live to see another sun-up.'

'Perhaps.' Gideon held his hands wide. 'But this all started when a card said you and Rusty had to face each other down with just one bullet apiece. That terrible position forced Rusty to do something equally terrible.'

'It doesn't excuse him.'

'It doesn't. But perhaps if that's how it all started, that's how it should end.' As Patrick shrugged, Gideon turned to Jack. 'Am I right in thinking that when you ask the cards, you give them three choices?'

Jack hefted the pack of cards in his right hand, then nodded.

'Yup. The choice you want has the greatest odds. The choice you'd prefer not to take has the lesser odds. And the least odds is the unthinkable.'

Gideon nodded, then folded his arms and drew himself to his full height.

'In that case, Rusty, then me, then Hannah will each fight a showdown with you. The cards will say who gets the gun with a bullet.'

'Go on,' Jack murmured, rocking his head to one side.

'A non-face card says only you get a bullet. A two-eyed card says both you and your opponent get a bullet. A one-eyed card says only your opponent gets a bullet.'

Jack rubbed his chin as he appraised Gideon, then turned to Patrick, who nodded. Jack pulled his gun. He punched out all but one bullet and hurled the gun to Leland.

Leland pulled his own gun and punched out the bullets while Jack fanned the cards and stalked to Rusty's side.

'Ask the cards,' he muttered.

Rusty reached out a shaking hand, then withdrew it. He blew on his fingers and stretched out the hand again, but the fingers were shaking even more than before.

'If you aren't feeling lucky,' Gideon said, 'I'll ask for you.'

Rusty gulped. 'No. I'll decide my–'

'I don't reckon you're a lucky man,' Gideon snapped. As Rusty turned to look at him, he set his firm gaze on Rusty's eyes and lowered his voice. 'Let me ask for you.'

For long moments Rusty glared at Gideon, then backed a pace.

'Then do it. But be lucky.'

Gideon smiled and paced to Rusty's side. He patted Rusty's uninjured shoulder with a friendly hand, then turned to Jack. He stared into his eyes as he pulled a card from the fanned-out pack and without looking at it, slammed it flat to his chest.

He turned and paced back to stand ten yards from Jack, then swirled round. With the tip of his finger, he lifted a corner of the card and glanced at it. He smiled and closed his eyes a moment, then showed Rusty, then everyone else the card.

A line of raised eyebrows and low whistles followed Gideon's revelation of his card – the Jack of spades.

'I got lucky,' he whispered as he turned the card to Jack. 'I got a one-eyed jack.'

Jack's mouth fell open. He muttered under his breath, then flared his one eye. Even his ruined orbit seemed to redden.

'How did you do that?' he grunted.

'Like I said,' Gideon murmured, holding the one-eyed jack aloft, 'I just got lucky. And you just got unlucky.' He glanced at Leland. 'Now give Rusty and Jack their guns and we can get this showdown started.'

'I ain't accepting that,' Jack roared.

'You have to,' Leland muttered. He hurled the unloaded gun to Jack's feet, then the gun with the single bullet in it to Rusty's feet. 'The cards ordered me to do plenty of dangerous jobs. It's tough luck, but you have to trust that Rusty's aim is bad. That's how we do things.'

'I don't have to,' Jack muttered, backing a pace as Rusty reached down and grabbed the gun.

'You do,' Gideon shouted. He folded his arms and faced Jack. 'Because if you don't, I'll tell Leland why you're so surprised that I got lucky and drew the jack of spades.'

Jack snorted, narrowing his one eye.

'It had to come up eventually. The cards

have just turned against me.'

'That isn't it.' Gideon held the card aloft. 'This card is clean. It looks as if nobody has drawn it before.'

'Nobody has.'

'But you have other cards that haven't been drawn and they're dirty.' Gideon widened his eyes and flicked the card to the ground at Jack's feet. 'It's almost as if this one wasn't in the pack before.'

Jack grabbed the card and shook it at Gideon.

'You cheated,' he snapped.

'I did. But so do you. You never ask the cards anything. You just cheat every time, then blame the result on random chance.'

Jack glared at Gideon, his face reddening by the moment.

'No!' Jack roared, the sound reverberating in the gathering night.

As one, Jack's men backed, any hint of their former arrogance gone as their shoulders slumped and they glanced at each other, then at Leland.

In open-mouth shock Leland stared at Jack. Then he dashed to Salvador's body and scrambled over him to get to his gun.

Jack rocked back and forth on his heels. Then, with his hands raised and held as claws, he charged Rusty. But Rusty hurled his arm up and blasted his sole bullet into Jack's chest, skidding him to a halt and spinning him back a pace. Jack clutched his chest, staggered another pace, then tumbled to the ground to lie on his back.

As Hannah screeched and dashed to Jack's side, Patrick dropped to one knee and with a burst of gunfire, sprayed lead across the remainder of Jack's men.

Don and Brady fell to the ground, clawing at their chests. Strang, Leland and Armstrong wavered a moment, then hurtled for the powder magazine.

Patrick blasted his last shot at their backs, but it ripped into the magazine's wall as they scurried inside.

Rusty dashed to Brady's side and kicked him over. He ripped his gun from its holster, then joined Patrick in kneeling and covering the magazine.

Gideon hung his head a moment, then wandered across the parade ground to stand over Hannah and Jack.

'Gideon,' Hannah whined, tears cascading down her cheeks as she looked at him. 'Help him.'

Gideon knelt beside Jack, noting the torrent of blood that was rapidly coating his shirt. He patted her shoulder and shook his head.

Hannah threw a hand to her mouth, then turned it over and bit the knuckle, stilling her shaking. She hung her head over Jack's face, but as his lips were moving, she placed her ear beside his mouth.

'Tell me what I want to hear,' he whispered.

'I can't,' she said. 'You always cheated.'

'I had to.' Jack lifted a limp hand with the jack of spades clutched between two fingers. 'But I guess you found the cards that weren't in the pack.'

'Yeah. The hand that lost you Amber.' Hannah sat back. 'Full house, jacks over kings.'

'Containing all the one-eyed cards.' Jack snorted. 'Wilton cheated and mocked me while he did it.'

Jack glanced at Gideon, who with an encouraging nod from Hannah, reached into his pocket and gathered the remaining cards from the fateful hand. He threw them on Jack's chest.

Jack nodded his thanks, then pointed to the side, asking Gideon to move away.

As Gideon backed out of hearing range, Jack gathered the cards and passed them to Hannah. He forced a grin and with a finger, beckoned her to place her ear above his mouth.

'Go to Black Rock and find Wilton Knox,' he murmured, his voice weakening with each word. 'At the right time, give the hand back to him.'

'And when is the right time?'

'When you've done to him what you did to

me.' Jack brushed a kiss against her cheek. 'Worm your way into his affections. Then, when his guard is down, double-cross him.'

Hannah lifted so that she could look Jack in the eye. 'I didn't double-cross you.'

'I don't care. All the women I've cared for have turned against me.' Jack's head keeled to the side, but with one last clawing swipe of his hand, he grabbed Hannah's collar and dragged her close. 'Just do it to him too.'

Hannah sobbed. 'I can't let you die thinking that I double-crossed you.'

'But you have. I saw what you did. Just call it blood money, or maybe...' Jack's one eye twitched as his voice faded to oblivion. 'Blood-gold.'

CHAPTER 19

As Hannah grabbed Jack's shoulders and cradled him to her chest, Gideon sauntered from them and joined Patrick and Rusty. He looked at each man in turn, noting that they were kneeling side by side, with none of the tension that had festered between them apparent.

'Are you and Rusty all right?' he asked Patrick.

Patrick glanced at Rusty, then hung his head a moment.

'Perhaps,' he murmured.

'He can't be,' Rusty said. 'That was a sham showdown. I was in no danger.'

'But you didn't know,' Patrick said, meeting Rusty's gaze for the first time in days without contempt. 'You were prepared to die. And that means you ain't no yellow-belly.'

'Suppose I ain't,' Rusty said, his jaw firm. He raised his eyebrows. 'But I won't know for sure until I get our gold back.'

'You mean, until *we* get our gold back.'

For long moments Patrick and Rusty stared at each other. Then, with the barest of nods passing between them, the two men rolled to their feet and headed across the parade ground towards the powder magazine.

Patrick hobbled and Rusty held his shoulder, but the backs of both were straight.

When they reached the magazine, they flanked either side of the doorway then, on the count of three, leapt through the doorway.

Standing ten feet away from Hannah and the prostrate Jack, Gideon watched their assault.

Gunfire blasted across the magazine, the small explosions bright in the darkened room. Through the doorway, he saw Armstrong leap to the side and walk straight into a low blast from Patrick that pole-axed him instantly.

With his legs set wide, Rusty stood in the centre of the room and blasted at Leland in the doorway to the second room. A returning shot ripped into his arm, but he shrugged it off, then pounded repeated gunfire at Leland.

As Leland plummeted to the ground, Strang ripped lead into Rusty's chest, spinning him to the ground.

Patrick scurried to Rusty's side and, kneeling over his body, fired at Strang.

The shot cannoned into the wall and Strang leapt at him. Patrick rocked back on his haunches and fired up at Strang while he was still in the air. The shot blasted through Strang's neck but even dead, Strang's momentum carried him on and bundled Patrick to the ground.

Patrick shrugged out from beneath Strang and leapt to his feet, his gun arcing towards each corner of the room, but moment by moment, the gunfire blasts echoed to nothing and all that remained was the evening calm.

Through the doorway, Gideon watched Patrick holster his gun and hunch over Rusty. Gideon gulped and glanced at Hannah who was matching Patrick's posture over Jack's body, but as he watched she pressed her head to Jack's chest and her body twitched as silent sobs rent through her.

Gideon sighed and stalked across the parade ground and into the powder magazine. In the doorway he stood a moment, enjoying the quietness, then checked on Rusty. The shot that had taken Rusty had ripped through his chest and would have killed him in an instant. Then he checked on Patrick, and he wasn't surprised to find he didn't have any additional injuries.

He knelt at Patrick's side.

'Can you do anything for Rusty?' Patrick asked.

'Nope.'

Patrick gulped. 'He was my friend. He died getting our gold back.'

'That wasn't the wound he was trying to heal.'

'I know.' Patrick smiled, then patted Rusty's shoulder. 'And I guess it was the same for me too.'

Gideon joined him and in silence they knelt on either side of Rusty with their heads bowed.

Only when a leg cramp forced Gideon to move did he slap Patrick's arm and point into the second room.

'Come on,' he said. 'Show me this gold that so many men have died over.'

Patrick led Gideon into the second room. The pile of bags Gideon had only seen once before was sitting by the back wall.

'If Jack hadn't stolen it from us,' Patrick said, 'nobody needed to die.'

'Perhaps, but I've never seen the attraction of gold myself.'

Patrick snorted. 'You mean you don't want a share for your help?'

'Nope. There are more important things in life.' Gideon frowned and glanced through the doorway into the darkening parade ground beyond. 'And if you haven't got those other things, who needs gold?'

Patrick sneered. 'When you haven't got the other things, gold compensates you.'

Gideon tipped back his hat, but the events of the last hour had blasted all enthusiasm for an argument from him and instead he dragged a blanket into the centre of the room, then deposited a bag on it.

One-handed, while still clutching his chest with the other hand, Patrick joined him in dragging the bags from the wall.

When the bags were in a pile, Gideon sat against the wall and watched Patrick check that all the gold was there.

Patrick grunted his acceptance of his bag count and pulled up the corners of the blanket, ready to bundle the bags together, but then with his brow furrowed, he lowered the blanket and hefted a bag.

'Wait a minute,' he murmured.

'What's wrong?' Gideon asked, rolling to his feet.

Patrick tossed the bag from hand to hand. 'This just doesn't feel right.'

He threw the bag to the ground and with a clawing finger, ripped it open. He peered inside, then stalked into the doorway where the early evening glow just provided enough light to see by. With his brow furrowed, he poured the contents on to the ground.

A pile of light dust grew.

'Whoa,' Gideon shouted. 'That's a bit reckless after all your trouble.'

'Don't worry yourself,' Patrick grunted, rolling back from the bag to deliver a swiping kick to the dust pile. 'This ain't gold dust. It's just dirt.'

Patrick dashed to the centre of the room and ripped open another bag, then another. He poured both bags on to the floor. In a frenzy he kicked and hefted bags, hurling them in all directions, kicking and tearing at the cloth until he flopped down to sit on the accumulated pile of dirt, clutching his ribs.

'All dirt,' Gideon whispered, unable to stop a smile twitching his lips.

'All dirt,' Patrick grunted. He glanced at Rusty's body with something more than just loss etched into his face.

Then Gideon and Patrick shared a long stare.

Gideon was the first one to wince. With his arms wheeling for more speed, he dashed into the parade ground, Patrick hobbling along behind.

In the parade ground, Jack's body lay on its own.

'Hannah!' Gideon screamed, but his cry echoed to nothing across the parade ground.

CHAPTER 20

Gideon dashed to the officers' quarters, then round the powder magazine, but long before he'd checked all the buildings, he knew that she'd gone.

When Gideon had completed a circuit of the fort, Patrick still stood outside the powder magazine. He'd dragged Rusty's body outside and stood over it with his head bowed.

Gideon joined him. 'Seems like she didn't need my help, after all.'

Patrick nodded. 'She was just a whore and she took the best price one ever got.'

'Her name is Hannah,' Gideon muttered, then sighed. 'But she can't have got too far if you want to go after her.'

Patrick tipped back his hat and raised his head.

'I don't. You were right. She's welcome to the gold. Sometimes you just have to settle for what you've got.'

'You letting her steal your gold?'

'Rusty and me got some of it back. It ain't enough to make me rich. But it's like you said, if you got somebody in your life, who needs gold? And I got a family to go back to.'

'You got it right there, Patrick.'

'Besides, I got a feeling she was the most formidable foe in this fort and I don't fancy my chances against her.' Patrick winked,

214

then turned and bent over Rusty's body. 'Now leave me. I have a friend to bury.'

Without complaint, Gideon left Patrick, but he still wandered around the fort, confirming that he was unable to help any of Jack's men or Salvador's followers.

Despite his joking promise to Salvador that he was accompanying him merely to bury the bodies, he only dragged them all into the powder magazine. By the time he'd moved the last body, the last sliver of brighter sky was coating the western horizon and Patrick had already plodded from the fort with Rusty dangling over his horse.

One last time Gideon glanced around the deserted compound, then headed for the stable and mounted his horse. With his head bowed, he rode through the gate and away from Fort Clemency.

Once he was on the open trail, he headed east towards a town called Destitution and a saloon called the Belle Starr.

He'd ridden for two miles when, at the crest of the first large hill, he narrowed his eyes and slowed his horse.

A rider sat astride the trail on the next hill, the form silhouetted against the night sky.

Gideon narrowed his eyes, but it was too dark to see anything other than the slightness of the form. Still, a smile spread.

It had to be Hannah.

But he continued at the same sedate pace as before. Closer to, he saw the pile of empty bags she'd dropped on the trail and atop them rested a mound. In the dark the mound was colourless, but as far as Gideon was concerned, it was clearly gold-dust.

Gideon pointedly kept his gaze from the mound and stared at Hannah.

'I thought you'd headed west?' he asked as he drew his horse to a halt.

Hannah shrugged. 'I got to thinking about what you said.'

'Any particular part? I said plenty to you over the last few days.'

'Pretty much all of it.'

Gideon nodded and glanced down at the mound.

'But you stole the gold.'

'I did. It took some effort, but I've become skilled at squirrelling away money and hiding it in places nobody can find.'

'Suppose you have.' The mound again drew Gideon's gaze. A breeze rustled the top. A flurry of dust spiralled away. 'But keeping it in the open like that isn't sensible.'

'It isn't.' She glanced around at the surrounding hills, their outlines etching the night sky. 'But I figured the dust came from the mountains. It can return there in its own time.'

Gideon tipped back his hat and blew out his cheeks.

'You don't want it?'

'Nope. The things you'll let people do to you for money have ruled my life. I don't want to be that person any more.'

Gideon looked down at the mound again, then tore his gaze away.

'If you don't want it, I ought to tell Patrick.'

'Will it make him any happier?'

'Perhaps not.' Gideon sighed. 'But if you don't want the gold, what do you want?'

Hannah smiled, her teeth bright in the dark.

'I enjoyed helping Patrick to mend.'

For the first time, Gideon let himself smile.

'I can help you develop that skill.'

'I hoped you might.' Hannah turned her horse from the mound and pointed east. 'Come on, before that gold changes my mind.'

She turned her horse and trotted down the slope.

Gideon hurried after her.

'You'll make a fine carer,' he said when he drew alongside. 'You won't regret this. Destitution is a poor excuse for a town, but I'm sure that...'

She turned in the saddle and smiled. 'I reckon that Black Rock might be a better place to start afresh. Neither of us needs to return to the Belle Starr.'

'But I was returning...' Gideon contemplated Hannah's welcoming smile. 'Black Rock it is.'

With that, Gideon rode in contented silence, but at the next hillock, a breeze rustled through his hair and he glanced over his shoulder.

The mound was disintegrating. The dust swirled into the air, with the starlight rippling through it. Inch by inch, the gold returned to its home.

Gideon gritted his teeth and tore his gaze away.

Hannah chuckled. 'Stop looking over your shoulder and look forward, then this will be a whole lot easier.'

'Yeah. But I can't help thinking that we'll have to survive until we get started in Black Rock. And that might take some time.'

Hannah licked her lips, but then threw back her head and ripped out a peal of laughter.

'Don't worry. It'll be an adventure.'

Gideon nodded and took a deep breath.

'On this adventure, do you think we will

ever ... that we will...'

Hannah turned to face him. 'Can't think that far ahead. For now, I just want to learn some new skills in a new town.'

'I understand.'

She fluffed her hair. 'And you might have competition in such a fine town. I might catch the eye of a prosperous gambler.'

'You might.' Gideon sighed. 'But whatever you decide, I'll still be there for you.'

'I know,' Hannah whispered.

Gideon smiled. One last time he slowed his horse and glanced over his shoulder.

The mound on the previous hillock was now only half its former size.

Although the dust sparkled in the starlight, Gideon was surprised that it still resembled the dirt Hannah had planted in Patrick's bags.

He shrugged and hurried after Hannah.

This Large Print Book, for people
who cannot read normal print,
is published under the auspices of
THE ULVERSCROFT FOUNDATION